BIG ISH

By

James J. Hill III

This story is based on actual events and real people. There was a great deal of research that went into telling the truth as best I could find. Some scenes and characters were created to fill in what could no longer be found.

James has also published other novels, including "When the Dandelions Sing," along with "Phoebe's Heart of Stone," as well as "The Gift of Life, Plus One," and most recently, "The Forgiving Path to the City of Springs."

This story was written for my family, to share a small history of people and events that were mostly forgotten for many decades, but will now have a chance to be remembered and passed down.

Special thanks to the following people who continue to help with my editing:

Flora Poloway

Amy McCormick

Amy Wolverson

And a thank you to my father, James J. Hill Jr., for remembering Ishmael's name, who he was, and for providing a base for which to start this story.

CONTENTS

One man, living as a small grain of sand in an old hourglass through time, can mean very little to the years that follow his life when that time runs out. How could that one simple man lose so much, and struggle so desperately to just live a life worth remembering for those he loved, but somehow, still be remembered a hundred years later for that life?

He most certainly did not ask for this life in the way someone asks for a pleasant favor. "It was just the way it was meant to be", he thought to himself many times over the decades. All he was doing was trying to carve out a small piece of quiet history for himself, for a life he was forced to live, and for those around him that he loved unconditionally. A spot in a small shred of time that he could be proud of for just a moment or two, and that those who would follow him could look back on with simple pride and maybe a smile or two.

And love, well, he loved in a way only he could comprehend. It was not traditional by any means, and he often showed that by the many harsh mistakes he made throughout his life, but he promised himself that one day he would correct that and make better choices. One day, he would let those people most important to him feel his love through the way he lived, even if it were not under the most conventional of ways, because his life was anything but conventional.

Many people experienced hard times towards the latter part of the 1800s and the very early part of the 1900s. The country was not for the weak, and the harder you were, the more it seemed you had to prove your worth to get by. Many men wanted to get by without being noticed if they could help it. But then there were those few men who simply stood out among the herd, no matter how much they did not wish to. Those that were larger than life, and had the scars across their battered and stained bodies to prove it. Those that if you crossed them in any way, would remind you for decades to come, that you made an awful mistake that one time, and would never, ever forget it in two life times of if you were granted such a gift.

Ishmael Heald Junior was one such man.

To those that knew him best, he was known as "Ish". To those that spoke of him when he was fighting his way out of trouble using his massive, calloused hands and whatever else he could pick up that could inflict pain, he was known as "Big Ish". And for those that crossed his path in the absolute worst of ways, he was known as a horrible handful that the devil himself would be afraid to cross. Seldom was anyone able to match his raw, natural strength, pure heart, and dangerous intentions sometimes so fierce, you had to wonder if he was human at all.

Maybe he was misunderstood for the way he saw life through those sad, gray eyes he was born with. Or maybe he wasn't, and was just a hardened man, living in the reality of a brutal world that taught you to be hard, or die. Whatever it was, no one within reach was safe when he was having a fit of rage. Not friends, nor man or woman.

Not even the police of the times could contain him if he did not allow them to. For even those men who tried to arrest him for his crimes had wished they had not.

Cross him, and there was truly a violent hell to pay. Try to stand in front of him to prove your worth among your fellow men, and you were only begging for what was to come. He wasn't called "Big Ish" for nothing. By the time he was a full grown man, he stood just over six feet tall, and weighed 227 pounds of which most seemed to be muscle and bone. In those days, most men had trouble hitting the 5'6" range. Most men didn't weigh anywhere near 200 pounds and were lean as anything from all the work and walking of a typical day. He earned that nickname for certain, and one could understand why he was not to be tested.

Ish was born from strong roots. His father, Ishmael Heald Sr., worked for many years on the family farm in Delaware, tending to crops and animals from sun up until sun down, until the day an accident took his left foot from his young body. When that happened, instead of giving up, which was not an option for a man with both pride and a family to take care of, he found another means to support a wife and kids while earning an honest living.

Ishmael Sr. was born in the state of Delaware in 1836. By the time the Civil War was rolling through in 1863, he was a 27-year-old man, working as a furnace tender. They were the men who were in charge of setting up, operating, and ensuring everything went as intended, so that they could melt the metals they were using to specific temperatures.

But the loss of a foot rendered him unfit to fight for the union, and so he would continue to do his work as best he could, unless he was called on for something else. He was unafraid of work, war, or anything else that may present itself.

By the time he was 27, he had already fathered four of the five children he would have in his lifetime. Ish would be his youngest son, and the one his father would need to worry about the most. He had a brother, William, but their father knew he would not need to worry about that boy. William, although from the same stock as Ish, was also built very differently.

And so begins the story of what some might call a legend if they did not know better. But Ish was as real a man as any that walked the face of the earth. He was at times a grieving father, a terrible husband, a proud grandfather for sure, and a son to parents who wanted to give him the opportunities of a lifetime. He was troubled by a life he was dealt without his permission, but he never gave up trying and fought back with the force of three able-bodied men combined. He lived a life we will never need to experience and thank God for that! Because as I see all this mountain of a man had to endure time and time again, I know I could not have done it as well and as humble as he did. But somehow, he still managed to make a life worth forgetting in his mind, into a life worth remembering in my mind.

He would deal with such horrific losses, and unimaginable

fights throughout his life, that ended at times with sharpened axes being swung with ill intent, shots being fired in the deepest, darkest of nights, and goodbyes he never intended on having. There were police that tried to tame him, judges that had to decide how to slow him down, and family that just wanted to understand him.

This man, Ishmael Heald, was my great-great grandfather. And this? This is his story that I am honored to be able to share with you. It's not a tale of sharing a good man's troubled moments in an effort to defend the way he lived his life. Although I do believe he had a lot of good in him for certain, I also believe he battled vicious demons that at times took that good from his heart and attempted to tear him down from within. They just did not know the type of man they were dealing with, the intense fight he had in his blood, and the lessons he would teach with time, that allowed others to understand their own lives better, as I have understood mine.

Chapter 1

As the Civil War ended in April of 1865, the country went back into a rebuilding stage that would take many years to achieve. Families had been torn apart as an estimated 620,000 souls lost their lives fighting for either their beliefs, or because it was simply what you did at the time to prove your worth. Times were different for sure, and so were the men and women who lived in those times.

Ishmael Sr. and his wife, Bridgett, were hoping for more out of life than just getting by. By 1869, that opportunity came by chance. Ishmael had been offered a job north of his state, along the Schuylkill River in the town of Conshohocken, in the southeastern portion of Pennsylvania.

It would be a big move and potentially a difficult one for their growing family of now five children, but Ishmael thought that the opportunities with the Alan Wood Steel plant should be strongly considered after a lengthy talk with his wife, Bridgett, she ultimately trusted his judgement, and agreed to make the move to give their family a chance for something better.

Bridgett had come over to this country from Ireland on May 19, 1847, at the age of just 15 years old. The ship she traveled on was called the Kalamazoo and had moved many men, women and children over from both Great Britain as well as Ireland, and so she was no stranger to uprooting an entire way of living to attempt a new one. This move would be so much easier for her than her move across the ocean, and she hoped, even better.

They settled into a modest home that Ishmael was able to afford, with money he had received from the death of his father, Passmore.

Passmore Heald was only 38 years old, when while he was carrying a pail of water across the busy Reading Railroad just a short distance from the city of Philadelphia, he was hit by a locomotive. The newspapers of the times held back little, if anything at all, explaining that Passmore had one arm, as well as his head, severed completely from his body. That was in the year 1843, when Ishmael was just seven years young.

Ishmael was quickly tossed into the role of man of the house, and he took that role with great pride and seriousness, working as hard as he possibly could to ensure his family was cared for, despite his young age.

For the first few years, things were hard for the Heald family, but that was to be expected in a new town, with new folks surrounding you that you did not know. Most of the homes in the area they resided in were occupied by other workers in the steel industry, and these were not like normal men and their families at all. They were tremendously hardened, uncommonly strong, and durable men who knew the value of an honest day's work. But they also had a common issue as well. They enjoyed drinking whiskey, and when the whiskey ran out and could no longer be found, beer or wine would fill that void.

It was not uncommon to see a fight on most nights throughout the neighborhoods in and surrounding theirs, but you minded your business as best you could and allowed men to be men and to settle their differences as they did. The area was not built for the faint or weak, though. It would take people with strong backbones, and good hands to go with that, or at least a good mouth to make others feel as if you had the first two, to stand your ground.

The Heald family had come originally from Quaker roots, and those people were more pacifist than fighters by design, that is, until Ishmael's grandfather, Isaac Heald, came into the picture.

Isaac was born a Quaker, but during the year 1776, things changed for him, and drastically. He was first charged by his church with the crime of fornication, a very serious charge within the Quaker religion.

Unable, or perhaps, unwilling to defend the claim placed against him, Isaac was banned from the Quakers Meeting House, and so began a life very much outside the belief system of the Quaker religion.

During the start of the Revolutionary War, Isaac's sister, Elizabeth, was confronted at her home by a group of Hessians, in the Brandywine region of Chester County. Those men would taunt her and her family by stringing her husband up from an old apple tree and threatening to hang him over and over by pulling and then releasing the rope, trying to get a rise out of young Elizabeth. They entered her home and stole everything not nailed down to the floorboards, leaving her family with virtually nothing left but the walls and wooden floors. In an act of sheer defiance, she warned the brutal men when they told of their intentions to stay in the country for good, "You are only here to find your graves."

Isaac, upon hearing the news of what his sister and her family had to endure for hours, quicky enlisted in the Chester County Militia under Captain Joseph Mendenhall, and swore to his dear sister, she would have her revenge through blood, his or theirs.

Isaac died in 1822, well after the war had ended and the country was liberated from English rule through the fighting spirit of the men who yearned for freedom. He left a large plot of land to his son, Passmore, who was only 17 at the time, and had himself become the man of the house much sooner than expected.

From that point on, this line of humble men and women would no longer go back to the Quaker religion and their passive ways, and instead would harden themselves for survival, and become even stronger people than ever.

As Ishmael worked hard in the plant, he began to make a name for himself through his work ethic and his strong mind. It would be rare for anyone to outwork a Heald, so naturally, he was noticed.

But tragedy would also strike the family man who simply wanted to provide a better way of life for his young family. Both Elizabeth and Mary Ann, the two oldest Heald daughters, passed away prior to 1870. There are no records I can find to tell you of how they passed, unfortunately. I could create a story that they were stricken by a terrible illness, or perhaps the tough town of Conshohocken got the better of them, but I do not believe that would do them justice, and would only tell an untrue tale. So they simply did not survive the move as well as their parents had wished. And that was that.

His son, William, was a good, dedicated worker. He first attended school in Saint Matthews parochial school, and by the young age of 12, left to work in the iron and steel mill with his father. Afterwards, that same year, he moved on to work at the Albion Print Works Company, which happened to be one of the borough's first industries. He worked there until the year 1877, at which time he headed back to work with his father once again, but this time as a catcher and a roller.

William was good with people, very well-liked and respected by those that knew him or of him. He was able to avoid trouble at almost every turn, using his mind over his fist whenever possible. But when it did come to those moments where his mind was simply not going to do the trick to get him out of a situation, young William was not afraid to throw his hands up and dish out a little punishment in response.

His brother, Ishmael Junior, may have been from the same bloodline, but he was built very differently. He had a streak of Isaac running through him, and was without a doubt, a fighter before a talker. He seldom felt that problems were solved with words thrown to the air for someone to grab with their ears. He would much rather throw heavy hands at an issue with dangerous intentions, to see who was left standing at the end.

The first police report I was able to locate on Ishmael Junior was from November of 1877. Back then, he was known as "young Ish", as he was just 15 years old at the time but stood tall over the average height of an average man already.

Young Ish had been drinking with some friends all afternoon, and for a presumably unprovoked reason, decided to attack a 23-year-old man named Alexander Simpson of Conshohocken. His court papers list him as Ishmael Hale Junior and charged him with assisting to create a riot. For some unknown reason, the father of Alexander, John, had at first insisted Ish was one of the group of boys that attacked his son, but later, changed his mind after speaking with Ishmael Sr. and receiving monies to satisfy the damage done to his boy.

The courts decided to not accept the settlement between

the two men as their agreement, and proceeded with the case at hand, fining Young Ish $5.15 and two nights in the local jail. They wanted to let this young man know, this was not the path he should be taking to manhood and not one they would allow in their town. The hope was that they could deter young Ish from a life of hard, troublesome times, but it would fall on deaf ears.

And so began an understanding for Old Ish that his boys were very different from each other. He began to see that young Ish had some demons within that he would struggle with greatly, and a life of freedom from pain and trials was not in the cards for him. He would need to speak with his youngest son and remind him that life was hard enough without the distraction of booze and street fighting, but would he ever find a way to get his boy to listen to his fatherly advice, was the question at hand.

William tried to talk sense into young Ish, but it fell on deaf ears. He had a ferocious temper, and because of his size, was a danger to anyone within arm's length, regardless of age. If you happened to cross this kid, you would know for years to come that you made a grave mistake, and would most likely have a scar to prove it.

As time went by, Old Ish started to feel the strains of working those long hours deep into the night, and the aches and pains were becoming an everyday issue. He was no longer that boy, who at the age of just 7, was in charge of a family that looked up to him. He was in a town that demanded a lot from him, and things started to catch up to his aging body.

And those boys of his would begin to travel down two very different paths, but brotherly love would not leave, even when tested over and over. That mutual respect would remain. At least for the most part.

Chapter 2

* * *

"Ishmael Heald? You're up next", the judge shouted. This was something all too familiar to this man, but he still hated to hear those words coming from an authority figure who presided over men. It also meant that there was a great chance he would not have his liquor to drink for a period of time and would have to suffer through those withdrawals he hated so terribly, as they caused both his body and mind to suffer.

Just a few years before, young Ish had married a somewhat troubled Irish woman by the name of Grace Whoriskey, who was born on a small island known as Tory Island, one of the harshest areas to get to by sea, in the northernmost part of Ireland. She came over with her mother, one brother, and a sister, after her father and at least one of her other brothers had died in a terrible accident while fishing the brutal waters off the Island, that claimed many a soul before and would claim many more after. She, too, had her fair share of heartbreak, so when her husband was heading before the judge yet again for the same foolishness, all she could do was throw her hands up into the air in frustration. How did this man expect her to raise a family and provide for them, when he could barely support her as he promised he would?

But she watched as he was led away by the police and went back home to tend to their two small children, Mary Agnes, born in 1880, and William, born in 1883.

Ishmael had briefly entered the National Guard at the age of 20, just a month after William was born. He was adamant that his first boy be named after his brother and would hear no other names for options. That was that. But when young William was brought into the world, Ish decided to enlist to get away from what he saw as the difficult task of raising young children.

Grace felt alone more often than she expected, as Ish was either doing drills with his unit, working long harsh days as an iron and steel worker with his older brother and father, or pleading his case before a judge to have fines reduced because he did not have the money to pay anyway. Usually he had consumed enough liquor when he was being arrested, that he forgot what had even taken place to cause him trouble in the first place, which made his defense harder to come up with. He tried being honest once, and all that got him was harsh criticism from a cocky, old judge who seemed to want to make an example of him. That didn't sit well with Ish.

So went things for Grace, until eventually, just a few

years into their marriage, she told Ish she was done with his shenanigans and was leaving. And she did, even though she was concerned with how she would make it on her own in such a harsh environment.

Ishmael found himself wondering where he would live as well now that his small rental on the east side of Norristown was no longer his to live in. Grace made sure of that, as she had a job to do now without her husband by her side. She would be damned if she was going to let this man interrupt that and cause her even more turmoil.

But Grace also had issues of her own. She had a hearty Irish temper, and seldom found herself in the company of decent people. Times were rough, and the towns they lived in were unforgiving on even the toughest of folks. But she was accustomed to tough conditions and knew she could make anything work, outside of her marriage of course.

The 1880's were difficult times for the Heald family, as no matter what they thought life should be, they just could not find a way to get the results they wanted for themselves and their kin. So any miniscule gain seemed to evaporate over and over again, making both Ishmael and Grace wonder what they had done to deserve such a horribly difficult time for simply trying to live.

Ish started to bounce back and forth between three areas that allowed him to find work and a place to lay his head at night; the borough of Conshohocken, the town he was moved to as a young boy, Norristown, the town he lived in when he married Grace, and Lancaster, where life would change for Ish forever.

After his marriage died in Conshohocken, Ish became a wanderer, going from job to job in search of mills that needed strong men to fill orders. They were more commonly known as "Tramps" for their constant moving around.

Wherever he was needed, Ish would travel, mostly by way of trains and then on foot. The trains would become a very important part of moving easily around for him, but they would also prove to be life altering, as Ish found out in November of 1889.

Between the towns of Columbia and Marietta, PA, Ishmael had attempted to quickly board a train for the purpose of stealing a ride back to his hometown of Conshohocken for the week, and for his unfortunate luck, he had been drinking a little too heavily into the afternoon. On his attempt to board the rapidly passing train, Ish slipped while trying to grab ahold of one of the open cars as it was passing by, and fell beneath the trains metal wheels that were rotating along the tracks.

Letting out a blood-curdling scream, Ish laid on the cold tracks that cold November day, unable to move himself to a safer place, and he waited. For what, he had no idea to be honest. Sobering up was not going to pleasant. The irony was that it was the alcohol that landed him in this predicament to begin with and now was his only source of comfort for the time being. He knew, however, that when the alcohol left his bloodstream, he would be in incredible pain.

Ish had no idea how long he had lain there, when at

about 8 pm, he finally heard a noise in the distant dark night. He heard a man's voice approaching where he now lay in terrible agony, but Ish was still a little too drunk to care much.

"Hey there, what are you doing there?" A man later identified as Track-walker Snyder asked.

Track-walkers were those men that strolled miles and miles along the train tracks, looking for any type of debris or obstructions that needed to be moved, and ensuring a safe passage was ahead for the trains that ran back and forth along those rails. Ish's now former brother-in-law, Dennis Waters, would go on to become one of the nation's top trackwalkers, accumulating some 111,000 plus miles of walking by 1911.

"Mind your damn business, and let me be", Ish scowled in reply.

As Snyder got closer, he could see with the light of his oil lamp light, the making of a large man laying down on the tracks, with a massive amount of blood spilled out all about him. The man appeared to have a mangled right leg, and Snyder could only assume it was a result of locomotive No. 346 running over it earlier that day.

"What the hell are you doing there? What are you up to? You are a mess, sir. Your leg..."

But Ish was saucy, and seemed to not have a care in the world that help was here for him and he would be pulled from his predicament and hopefully, helped to a better, safer place where he could be assessed. He screamed and cussed at the man who was simply trying to help this tramp off the tracks.

Eventually, though, Snyder was able to secure some help from others, and Ish was taken to Columbia, where upon examining his terrible condition, they had no choice but to amputate his right leg six inches below his knee.

Once that horrible procedure was finished, he was immediately sent by freight train to the city of Lancaster, which Ishmael had spent many years off and on working and traveling through. He was then moved to the county hospital, still mostly intoxicated because of the large amount of booze he had consumed. The ride was anything but pleasant across the stone roads, as he was placed in an old, worn stretcher, hoisted up to a waiting wagon that was used for carrying the mail through the city during the day, and then shuffled off to the hospital.

The people of the city were astonished at both this man's condition, and the means with which he was traveling to the hospital in their town.

One man was heard shouting from the street,

"We have no better way of helping our sick and wounded? This city should be ashamed of itself."

Another cried,

"That poor man. Why, he looks as if he has little chance to make that trip to the hospital at all."

But the men had a job to do, and so they largely ignored the callers from the streets and focused on the task that was at hand. It was hard enough having to deal with the drunken nature of the fool who fell from a railcar.

By the following morning, Ish had realized the severity of his condition, as the liquor he consumed was finally leaving his body, allowing him to see clearer just what shape he was in.

At first, it was thought with the amount of blood he had lost, that this man would not survive through the night. The amputation was painful, but necessary to give him a fighting chance. The doctors gave him a slim chance at survival, even for the man's size and strength. But they did not know Big Ish well. It would take a heck of a lot more to take this mountain down. He was not the type of guy to let a limb removal slow him at all, and so he miraculously made a good recovery over the next few weeks, just enough that he could go back home to Conshohocken to visit with his family, this time, without having to steal a ride.

Chapter 3

* * *

"Dad? What on earth happened to your poor leg?" Mary Agnes asked.

She was just nine years young but was already a caring and concerned girl. She was curious as all hell about everything and anything, too.

Ishmael left home fully intact and came back a bit broken from what his children could recall. Although he was not around most days, they knew when their father was suffering more than usual, even if he tried desperately to hide his pain and humiliation.

"Don't you worry, my little one. It'll take a lot more than some stupid metal beast to break this man's spirit. Rest assured, Mary Agnes, your father is perfectly fine", he smirked back at her.

Grace would not see Ish on this return. She had heard that he was badly injured, but overall she also knew she needed space from him, and that was something her children knew as well. Ishmael had resolved himself to the fact that his marriage was over for certain, but he had those two children, Mary Anges and William, to enjoy when he could. His duties did not die as the marriage had.

William was different. He was a mild-mannered boy and did not do well in the spotlight. He mostly kept to himself, and unlike Ish, he was not a man of large stature. William did not enjoy fighting with his hands and preferred to stick to himself most of the time.

His kids were as different from one another as he was from his own brother, William.

"William, you all right? Come here, boy", Ish called to his son.

William slowly went over to where his father was seated and sat down by his side. Ish picked him up with his calloused hands, sat him on his lap, held his boy, and smiled at him. He wanted William to have no fear of how his father was. Ishmael put his head up high, lifted Williams to meet his, and reminded him,

"Don't you worry none. I have a lot left to give this world. I'm good, William. I'm good."

Mary Agnes was more curious and gently walked over to Ish. She was staring at his right leg, wondering what was beneath the cloth that seemed to not match the other side. Ish pulled it up to expose his wooden leg for her to see. It astonished young Mary Agnes as she had never seen the likes of it before. She certainly had known her grandfather, or Old Ish as everyone called him, lost a foot, but this was the entire bottom half of his leg. How her father was still smirking through his story of how it came about, amazed her to no end.

Ish recanted the story to his children, and soon after finishing, his own brother, William, appeared. He loved his niece and nephew, and always had with him a small piece of candy to give out whenever he stopped by for a visit.

William had been married to the same woman, Mary Shaw, for nine years now. They had four daughters by this point, and sadly, just two years prior, had lost their only boy almost to the day of what would have been his first birthday.

When Ish saw his brother enter the room, he knew he was getting a lecture of sorts. It's just how it went with the brothers. Ish would mess up something awful, and William would sit and try to talk sense into the man who never seemed to get it right, which, to this date, had not worked to change a thing. But William wasn't ready to give up on his younger brother just yet.

"Uncle William! Come. See what father did to his leg. Look, it's not there!" Mary Agnes said.

"I see that. Well, now what happened here?" William joked back, as he clearly knew the story already.

Mary Agnes was smart enough to know when someone was joking with her, but she wanted to tell him about the story, at least the version of the story she was told. She was only told of the part where her father slipped and fell beneath the car as it was passing by. She had been spared the honest truth of her father being so drunk that he barely knew what he was doing that evening. She did not know that he tried fighting with the track-walker who was simply performing his duties that night. Or that he screamed horrible curses towards each and every man and woman who came to prevent the great amount of blood he leaked out onto those cold tracks from costing him his life.

"Mary Agnes, give us a moment, will ya?" Ish asked.

She went over to hug Uncle William, and then, with her brother by her side, went out across the street to visit with some friends from the neighborhood who were making noise in the street.

"William, listen. I don't need any of your words of wisdom right now. Hear me? Let it be." Ish said.

But William was not one to just let it go because he was asked to. He was proud of his brother's hard work ethic, but entirely frustrated with how reckless everything else in his life was. How could a Heald, who came from such strong stock, throw brutal caution to the wind, time and time again? He was going to kill himself one of these days if he did not get his life in order and listen to advice he needed to hear, even if he knew the right from wrong already.

"Listen here Ish. You have those two darling children to think of. Why not give that booze a break for a while and see if you can get your affairs in order some?" William asked.

"It will always be there for you when you need it here and there", he continued.

When William talked, it had the stiff tone of an authority figure, and although he was older than his younger brother by two years, Ish did not see that as any reason to listen to him. He didn't heed his father's warnings, his mother's pleas, nor was he going to listen to another common steel worker telling him what he needed to do.

Although William was strong, he was not Ish strong. So beating sense into him was simply not an option. He would need to figure out a better way, but so far, nothing was working. Not even his words of wisdom seemed to make much sense as he spoke them. If a train cutting off your limb didn't work, what else could you say to a fella to get him to wake up and make changes to his day?

"Those kids are just fine. Grace sees to that. I send money home when I can, and I see them each time I get back to this area. What more do you expect from me?" Ish replied.

William knew it was senseless to even continue to give his brother advice. So instead, he decided to sit by his side and just talk about steel for a few moments. It seemed to be the one thing they could agree on. Whatever he could use as a catalyst to connecting to his brother, was just going to have to do for now.

"Want a drink?" Ish asked.

Before William could even answer his brother, Ish had pulled out a flask of whiskey, took a swig for himself, and passed it over to his brother.

If you saw these two men sitting there, you would know they were kin. Both had thick, sandy blonde mustaches. Both had well defined upper bodies, built to withstand the rigors of a harsh working environment with heavy metals worked between their hands. Both had a strong look of determination, even if for very different reasons. The fact that Ish was larger was simply the way it was.

William was just glad his brother was home for a while, and alive at that. Things could have been much worse for the brothers. They could be planning a funeral instead of sharing a flask of whiskey. At least for that, both were happy. But what about the next time? What if Ish was not so lucky, and whatever came next ended differently for the brash man?

"How's that hag Grace making out anyways?" Ish questioned with a smirk.

William knew it bothered Ish that their marriage lasted such a short amount of time. When Ish first met Grace, it was he that said he found the girl of his dreams and would marry her and make a proper woman of her. So to see him lose her over his profuse drinking and that nasty temper of his, was tough to watch.

"Oh, Grace, she's all right. Haven't seen much of her lately, but the kids say she's getting along", William answered back.

He was trying to avoid a lengthy talk about his former sister-in-law, as Grace was back to dating again. The last thing he needed was for his brother, Ish, to find out and go clobbering some poor soul over the head with those large hands of his, or worse, a club.

The brothers sat back and talked, and occasionally one would ask about their kids, or speak about how their father, Old Ish, was making out. The talk didn't lean much on the fact that Ish was now considered a cripple, because, well, in both of their minds, he was still not. William knew that even with one leg, he still had a leg up on just about any man in town, or elsewhere.

Mary Agnes crept back into the home quietly, trying to gain a listen to what her father and uncle were discussing with the kids outside of the house. Her curiosity was always raining down wherever she was, and Ish loved that about her.

Just outside, the town of Conshohocken was buzzing with noise. Things were rough for sure, and it seemed as if nothing was going to slow down the trouble coming in. It was mayhem at times, and Ish was always worried for the safety of his two children. He made William promise him that in his absence, he would keep one of those good eyes of his out on the kids. It was the least William could do for family.

And William did just that. He watched over those youngins as if they were his own. He knew his brother would be leaving town again soon, and that in doing so, he would not be able to keep him in line. He worried for Ish, not because he was afraid anyone was going to get over on him, but more for the fact he would one day get a letter that his younger brother had finally met with someone or something his equal, and he would no longer have that upper hand. And that then, they would bury him before his time.

Chapter 4

* * *

Within a year, Big Ish was back at it again. He traveled to Lancaster County to start working at the furnace, and his drinking was as heavy as ever, although if you asked him, he would surely tell you different.

On November 22, 1890, Ish had what seemed like a minor disagreement with a man named Robert Templeton. Robert was also a laborer in the same trade, working in the same capacity as Ish, and was employed in the same. A conflict occurred over an Irish lady they both fancied, and Robert smacked Ish sharply in the back of his head to thwart his advance toward her, no doubt under the influence of a massive amount of whiskey.

Ish swung his body around in one swift, smooth motion, clocked Robert upside the right side of his head, which caused Robert to drop to the ground below like an old sack, rendering the man unconscious for several minutes. Ish never ran, and instead, opted for the police to come so he could claim his side of what transpired. For what it was worth, he felt he was justified in clocking that son-of-a-bitch, and so naturally, he did as he saw fit.

Come Monday morning, both parties had sobered up well enough in a jail cell, that they arranged for their disagreement to be squashed as men often did, and the assault and battery filed on Ish was dropped so that he could be on his way.

The constable who first arrested Ish made mention to the fact that he ought to be more careful and to knock off that foolishness.

"Big fella, I know you have that great strength of yours to throw about, but come one of these times, you are going to find that one leg of yours to be a downfall to you for certain."

Ish simply cracked a smile as if he knew something no one else did. He never said a word, and instead just turned away, walked out the door he was dragged into, and went back to perform the work that was still waiting for him. His work was completed whether he was mostly sober or mostly not. Most times he would drink whiskey well into the evening, or even the early morning hours if midnight came calling just a little too fast, he slept a few hours in a raggedy tent or makeshift shanty, and then somehow woke before the sun, had a bite to eat before dressing, and would head back to the factory to get started all over again. He did not dare stay in bed hungover, nor did he struggle with his duties, despite the best efforts of the alcohol the night before to render him useless. For that, Ish was both marveled and sought out for his ability to work through just about anything, and the men in charge would turn the other way if they needed to. Besides, they never cared for the personality of a man. It was all about the productivity.

That year and the following, there would be many more tussles with men and even on occasion or two, woman, depending on how the incident unfolded.

On April Fool's Day, 1892, Ish was helping a woman by the name of Kate Gaul move her items from her home for a relocation she was making just to the other side of the city. They started drinking early on in the mid-morning, consuming a considerable amount of whiskey between the two. Whiskey was Ish's drink of choice as it was cheap and plentiful, so naturally he gravitated towards it.

Ish started to get into a playful mood by late that afternoon and decided it would be a fun idea to throw her furniture around haphazardly. A passerby by the name of Henry Leonard heard the commotion and tried to induce Ish to stop his silly actions immediately and act like an adult should. He was a man who did not appreciate the tramps in the area and had no issue telling them how he felt about their presence. That did not go over well with Big Ish, and he began to walk over to where the man had stopped on the street, swearing from the start to the moment he landed in front of this now nervous man.

He hit Henry with his left hand, knocking him over his own feet, and then decided to grab a wooden club with his other hand, and hit the man over the head a second time. Not feeling like he had done enough to change this fella's mind to mind his own business, Ish for some reason decided to bite Henry on the cheek, drawling a considerable piece from the man's face, and causing him to scream out a horrible sound of agonizing pain that was heard through the entire block.

Ish was once again arrested for assault and battery, locked up pending a hearing, and sentenced to five days in the city's jail. When he returned to work, most of the men knew what had happened that day. Word got around when "Big Ish" was handling his business. It was hard to hide when you stood out among other men, and Ish wished at times that he had a better handle on his anger and drinking, but that devil seemed to consume him with each drink that coursed through his veins and each blow he struck, cursing him to continue with the beatings. It was as if it was hopeless to expect any different from himself. He could barely get through a week without blind rage raining down on him, and he began to wonder why he could not be more like his brother William. How could he be the parent William was to his kids if he could not control his own damned body and mind when he needed to most? They took over with a ferociousness that most could never fathom, even for the times.

For his part, William continued to build a name back home at the iron works he stayed at. He would come home each evening instead of hanging out with the steel boys, drinking away their lives into the dark nights. He never thought that was a good, smart use of his time. William had seen what it was doing to his younger brother, and knew he had to show his kids, and perhaps Ish's as well, that there was a better way to live and more to gain from good, moral decisions.

Grace was doing odd jobs until she was hired as a housekeeper for a man named Amos Alexander, another well-known steel worker from Conshohocken. Although William had his doubts that she was truly employed by this man, but rather fancied him.

Amos was well known for almost the same reason as Ish. He was as tough a steel iron worker, who had a grand taste for cheap whiskey, and a red temper that rose at the drop of a hat. Few people dared get in his way when a full head of steam was coming off Amos.

He took Grace in as well as both of her children. William preferred to be with his father, but with Ish working in Lancaster, there was really no way possible for him to go and be with him. It wasn't that he didn't like Amos. It was more that he felt something was different about the man his mother decided to board with, but he could not place his finger on it just yet.

Mary Agnes seemed to like everyone, so for her, she saw life as moving just fine. Nothing really bothered her, and she wanted her mother to be as happy as she could be, so she went along with whatever was working for Grace.

William hesitated to tell his brother about Amos. Not until he knew a little more about him first, and even then, he still had great hesitation. His fear was that Ishmael would come back to Conshohocken, see this tough iron worker holding on to his children, and immediately head into a rage, pitting two stubborn, red-tempered men into a fight that would surely kill one, if not both men.

No. He would keep it to himself and told both William and Mary Agnes to do the same. You didn't need to tell Grace to keep it to herself. She needed no more attention on her, nor did she need the trouble of her former husband causing all sorts of problems. Besides, she swore to William that she was simply working for him, and he offered her a room that would allow her to save some money for her and the kids to get a better, safer place.

Ishmael had troubles of his own with women. That same Kate Gaul that he was helping, had a thing for Ish, before he decided to throw her furniture about. The trouble was that she was still married, but that didn't seem to stop her from wanting more from him. Eventually, Ish decided to move in with Kate in a small home on Middle Street in Lancaster, despite her marriage to this other man.

Kate was not divorced but had left her husband some time ago. Ishmael was not keen on the idea of getting married again after seeing what had happened to him and Grace, so he decided this was the next best thing.

In July of 1893, there was a misunderstanding between Kate and another woman by the name of Sophia Hood. Sometime during the argument, Kate struck Sophia over the head with a parasol, causing Sophia to wither in pain, and in turn, report her and Ish to the Lancaster authorities.

Both were arrested that same day, and Kate was charged with assault and battery, as well as fornication for her time with Ish.

Ishmael was once again charged with fornication, a charge he was growing used to defending. The good this time, though, was that those charges were dismissed for her and Ish, except for the assault and battery charge she was arrested for. She was fined and ordered to not have any further contact with Sophia in any way.

That didn't last long, though, as Ishmael, as a tramp, was more into the traveling ways he had experienced for many years, going from place to place, working at different steel plants and furnaces, wherever they needed strong, able-bodied men.

He would head back home a few times a year, more careful this time when stealing a ride, and visit with his brother and father, while seeing the kids when he wasn't too deep into the bottom of a bottle. The good news was that while Ishmael was in Conshohocken, his brother was fairly successful at keeping him out of fights, even if it seemed a near impossible task. William had a way with people, including his brother, which amazed those around them.

It was simple, really. Ish respected William and didn't want to see a disappointment in his brother's eyes. He wanted William to see him not as the big, foolish, tough fighter that he was, but as a simple man, trying to find his way through this world he certainly did not ask for a place in, even if he didn't know what that was meant to look like.

By 1894, things began to grow more out of control for Big Ish. His ability to fend off any man was making him feel more and more invincible. He believed that no one could get over on him, drunk or sober. If locomotive No 346 could take his leg but not his soul, a normal man would not have a shot in hell.

So Ish would find his way into bigger issues back in Lancaster, which seemed to be how life was going to always be for him.

Chapter 5

* * *

Ishmael was drinking more heavily, and although he did not see the danger in that while in the act, when he woke up in those lonely, cold jail cells full of concrete and metal, he began to wonder why the devil had brought him the first drink to begin with. Was it the fact that he was raised in a town of hardened steel workers, who had little to do but fight and drink into the early morning hours to pass the time? Was it seeing his own father pick a drink up here and there to ease his mind, or those times he would steal a sip of whiskey when Old Ish was passed out for the night in his chair? He didn't know for certain, but what he did know was that he could not see a way to get over it.

Ishmael, for someone who seemed to always find trouble like a magnet, was actually very good at making friends. People enjoyed this giant of a man when he had no alcohol running deep through his veins. He was a pleasant man on most days, and when you needed a hand, there was no better person to ask.

It was as if he were two completely different men altogether. Sober, you wanted to sit with him and talk into the evening, reminiscing about family affairs, or a woman that had caught your attention the week before and the next time you swore, you would ask out.

But when he was drinking, this gentle giant became something completely untamable and impossible to predict. Even close friends had to worry about stepping on the wrong side of Ish, and even Ish regretted the truth in that. He simply could not understand the reason behind his alter ego and felt he ought to have a say in how that went.

In December of 1894, Ish was heading to a friend's house named John Herr. He did not know that John was away at the time, but a boarder named Henry Stroeble and John's wife happened to be home. Ish did not know Henry, but he had met John's wife on occasion, and when Henry invited Ish in for a drink, how could he turn that down?

Henry was also a steel worker, like Ish, and big for a man of his times. Not that it bothered Ishmael in the least. He was there to see a friend of his, and what harm could a drink or two do before he headed back to his home? None if he could keep the drinking in check.

They began by drinking terrible beer to pass the time, but by the time they had finished the supply at hand, the two men decided to finish the evening off with some cheap wine that was laying around the home. This turned out to be a bad combination, as it just got both these big men into a chaotic state of mind.

Starting off, it was the typical playful verbal jabs of men thrown back and forth between the men as men often do, but soon after, those words turned to much more when John's wife started to jab back harshly at Ish, telling him to be a man and stop acting as a child does. He grabbed at the woman and swore to her it was best for her to mind her business. That's when Henry grabbed the Ish's shirt, trying to turn the now angry man and get his large hands off his landlady, but that did not sit well with Ish. He was not one who enjoyed being tested by man or woman, so he pushed back at Henry with a force that sent the man tumbling down.

Up the street, a constable by the name of Nehr was coming home from a long shift. He heard such a great commotion, that he quickly ran down to see what the hell was causing this wild noise in the early evening.

When he arrived, he saw both Ish and Henry going at it blow for blow in the back yard. The two men were throwing hands and whatever else was nearby at one and other, with terrible intent on harming the other with a vicious purpose behind each strike. Ish was getting the better of Henry, having slammed him onto his back down to the hard earth, and he started raining down heavy lefts and rights onto the man's face.

Immediately, Nehr raced over to where the men were in an attempt to separate them, calling out that he was a constable acting in the line of duty for the city of Lancaster. He placed his hands onto Ishmael's broad shoulders to pull him off, and Ish grabbed Nehr, busting open his top lip, then threw the bettered constable across the snowy yard. He grabbed a wooden chair that was sitting nearby and broke it over Nehr's head. Then he grabbed a board that happened to be lying next to the chair in a pile of debris from construction going on at the Herr home, and slammed that into the constable's shoulder as well, nails and all.

When Ish went back to finish off Henry, Nehr found a wooden broomstick handle laying nearby, and began to hit Ish over the head with it as hard as he possibly could, in an all-out attempt to slow the big man down. After several blows, he finally was able to settle Ish down enough to comply, or so he thought.

Nehr was able to summon a patrol wagon to take Ish in, but before it arrived, he and Henry were going at it yet again. It seemed a second wind had kicked in for both men, and they decided to try it once more, which did not go well once again for Henry.

For the crime of fighting, public drunkenness, and hitting an officer of the law with an oak plank that punctured the shoulder of constable Nehr, Ishmael Heald was fined, made to stay the night in jail so that he could sober up, and released. Nothing more.

When he finally did sober up, he took full responsibility for his actions, apologizing to all parties involved, and telling the court that he truly meant no harm. Perhaps they believed him, or maybe they took pity on the man with just one good leg. It was clear he was a hardworking man coming from good stock as anyone could see, so the judge may have felt these men who were born of rough backgrounds and worked tirelessly through all conditions to provide for their families, just needed to blow off some steam. Even if it meant hurting others in the process. These were tough times and times like this required even tougher men.

Besides, it was getting close to Christmas, and Big Ish wanted to spend time back home with his family and to see his children. He had purchased a few small things for them from the company store not far from where he stayed, and if he were in jail, he would not be able to surprise them on Christmas morning.

Back in Conshohocken, things were rapidly changing as well. Mary Agnes was blossoming into a beautiful girl, and the men of the rough town were taking notice. William was worried about her, and desperately tried to keep her from the dangers the town had to offer. He knew men were only out for some trouble, and unfortunately, Mary Agnes seemed to favor the attention she was receiving, good or bad.

William knew that eventually, if things did not change, she would find herself at the very least pregnant, if not in the gravest of troubles, which she would surely regret.

"Uncle William, please don't worry. I know what I am doing, and besides, mother and Amos are always keeping a close eye on me," Mary Agnes said.

But William did not trust Amos. He knew from the other men in the steel business that Amos had issues of his own that he battled nightly. Not only did he have a vicious temper, but he also had a jealousy streak like no other man he knew. That was a terrible combination to have for anyone.

"Mary Agnes, do me a big favor, will ya? If you need anything, come to me. I know you have your mom and ol' Amos there but listen here. You come to me if you feel you need anything. I promised your father I would keep an eagle eye on you, and I always keep my promises," William replied with a wink.

She knew she could trust her uncle with anything, but she trusted her gut instinct, and Amos would never bring any harm to her. While he did holler at Grace a little more than she would like, her mother always told Mary Agnes that he meant well, was a good provider, and when he wasn't having a fit of rage, he was quite good to her and the kids. Not to mention, they needed a safe place to call home for now.

When Ishmael arrived back in Conshohocken in the winter of 1894, he was finally made aware of the living arrangements between Grace and Amos. He was not pleased, having known about Amos through the grapevine of steel workers throughout the counties they all worked in, but he also knew Grace had a right to do as she wished.

William was shocked by how well Ish took the news, and was even proud of his brother for understanding. Perhaps his brother was maturing more, and for this, William was optimistic.

The truth was that Ishmael knew he was absent more

than not and didn't like his kids growing up with just Grace to protect them. He knew Amos wasn't exactly the man he would pick out to be in his kids' lives, but he also knew if there was trouble, Amos would serve well as someone who could create enough chaos to stop it.

Ishmael spent the holidays at his father's home on Oak Street, in a row of homes commonly known as "Stone Row." He told his father about working out in Lancaster, and of how he planned to eventually move back when he had enough money saved. It was his eventual desire to come back and be closer to his children so that he could be a better father to them and watch as they grew.

Old Ish did not ask much about the trouble his son caused, as he knew he could do nothing about that. Instead, he focused on telling Ish Junior about the struggles he, too, faced growing up with an absent father who had died far too young, and how he worked hard to be the man of the house as was expected. Bridgett use to love that story, as she was proud of her husband for overcoming such terrible times and standing tall in the role he should never have had. But she had passed two years ago now, and that story was seldom told since.

When Big Ish went to visit his children, William and Mary Agnes, Grace was home with her now husband, Amos Alexander. This would prove to be tough for Ish, and his brother William begged him,

"Do not partake in any drinking of any kind, brother. Promise me, you hear? Be there for your children and your children alone," Wiliam pleaded.

Ish respected his brother's position and advice, and decided that he was probably mostly right. He knew if he could just keep his temper under control and focus on the kids, it could save him a night in jail and allow him to enjoy his kids that much more.

Mary Agnes was worried, as she knew both men well by now. Amos did not like her father at all and felt he had abandoned his children and treated Grace horribly over the years. Ish did not like Amos for many reasons as well, and at the drop of a hat, both men could easily decide to test the other one.

But Ish held his ground and entered the home to see Amos and Grace sitting there in the main room, with his two children running to the door to greet their father. He noticed nothing else but those beautiful children, with their eyes lit up, looking up to their father. It was all he cared for in the world at that very moment, and no one was taking that from him.

"I'm home," he told them.

Chapter 6

* * *

"Council, bring your first witness," the judge ordered.

Before the case was presented, the judge decided it was better to clear out the court room. He did not see any reason to have this turn into something that would potentially hurt a young girl or harm the career of a man who may or may not have done something terrible, depending on the outcome of the case presented before him.

But William had been right to worry about Mary Agnes as it turned out. That niece of his was so kind and naïve to the ways of the world and the people who walked it's dirt, but he could do only so much to ensure she was safe from the evils that abound.

By 1895, Mary Agnes had left the comfort of her home in the Norristown area where she lived with her mother, Grace, and Amos Alexander, she was lured into a life of exploring other options for herself in Wilmington, Delaware. She was but barely fifteen years old at the time, somehow feeling that she was capable of making great decisions in her life and needed no one's approval for any of them.

In June of that year, Mary Agnes was living in a house that ended up being raided by the city's police, on the possibility of high-end prostitution. She was suspiciously not there at the time, but several other females that were inmates of the same residence, as they called them, were rounded up and swiftly arrested. By this time, Mary Agnes was going by the name of "Trixy," in an effort to hide her true identity, in case she, too, was ever apprehended.

A private detective by the name of Richard G. Howard was one of the men who had gathered evidence for his brother, the Reverend, Dr. John H. Howard, in an effort to restore order and clean up the vice in his city, that had been plaguing it for some time now. Between the drug use and the prostitution, the residents of the city had had enough and wanted change and order, and the Reverend was going to push for that change.

Richard was considered to be a spy for the movement heading off the investigation, but had no authority from the state of Delaware, nor the city of Wilmington, to act in such a capacity. It was considered somewhat of a political move to disparage the other side, and their failed efforts to clean up the city they lived in. The police and commissioner were slammed for allowing this to go on for so long and not doing their duty to clean up the city or to enforce the laws that were enacted.

The Reverend gave a sermon about "high-toned houses

for high-toned boys and men" to enjoy themselves. He said these illicit places were traps for the best boys in the city to visit and lose their manhood and self-respect at the same time.

Further during his speech, he spoke of the police commissioner, who at one time had been a saloon owner himself, and wondered how he could take on such a job, knowingly having to deal with those he was once in business with. It would be a black mark for sure on the commissioner and the city authorities.

After the sermon, Richard and his brother were set to leave the church and head towards home to enjoy lunch with their families. They were stopped prior to leaving by uniformed officers who informed Richard that he was being placed under arrest for the act of fornication with a girl just fifteen years of age.

Richard was shocked and according to the newspaper reports, turned several shades of color, perhaps embarrassed, or more probably scared out of his mind for what was to come.

When Mary Agnes returned to Wilmington, she was also rounded up by police and arrested for the crime of prostitution in a home that catered to men of money and served liquor without a license.

On her arrest, she accused Richard of having intercourse with her on a several occasions, which he believed was an elaborate trap to thwart the purpose of what he and his brother were trying to do. The problem was that there were witnesses to his acts that placed him in the home where Mary Agnes was at the time.

He was removed and taken to police headquarters where he was placed in a jail cell and charged with the crime at hand. He faced a fine of one thousand dollars and up to seven years imprisonment, based on the recently passed act stating that the age of consent was eighteen years of age.

The topic was openly discussed by the citizens throughout the community, who were either shocked by the accusations, or had no time to believe that this man, the brother of a well-respected Reverend, had at any time broken any laws. After all, he was a married man with six children living at home, and would have so much to lose if the accusations were proven to be true.

It was then brought to the attention of Reverend Howard that he, too, was being arrested, but he did not go as quietly as his brother. He remarked to the arresting officers,

"I understand you have trumped up charges against us and you had better drop them."

The arresting office in charge, McVey, simply replied,

"Mr. Howard, we are not the law, but simply the instrument of the law. If there is to be any dropping, it must be after the evidence is heard."

Grace was informed of what was happening, and along with Amos, headed south towards Wilmington to be with her daughter. While she did not know why Mary Agnes had left town, she was certainly aware now, with the charges both against her daughter and this man named Howard.

She was fearful of what Ish may think once he found out what had transpired while she was supposedly in her care. She knew he was not one to steer clear of anyone, including the law. He had so many brushes with police officers in the past, but this would be different. This was a well-known city with a large force and prominent men in charge, and Ish would not get the same treatment as he had in the past within the more rural areas where he was usually arrested.

Before she left, she contacted William to let him know what was going on, and to see if he would be the one to advise Ish on the findings, in a way that would keep the big man as calm as could be, considering the circumstances. William of course agreed but had no idea of how he would even keep his brother calm during this time. Nor would he expect him to be.

It so happened that Ish was on his way back to Conshohocken to visit just about the time all of this was going down. William met his brother at the train station and welcomed him home with a brotherly hug.

"Ish, it's good to have you back. How the hell ya been?" William asked.

Ish knew something was off, as his brother was not good at hiding when he was being pained by something.

"William, what is it? What happened?" Ish asked confused.

William did not want to tell him just then, because there were a lot of folks around, and he did not want to upset his brother before he had a chance to relax a bit and get out of the public eye. This was a private, family matter that was surely going to open to the public at any time. It had begun to find its way to the newspapers, and the story was being told without holding back any of the details, including Trixy's real name. Ish would know his daughter was arrested for prostitution, and how could a man be expected to handle such terrible news?

When they arrived back at William's house, he sat his brother down and began to tell him the story, at least the one he knew based on the limited information he had gathered. Without saying much, and without storming out in a rage that was partially expected, Ish stood up, looked at William, and told him he needed to go to Wilmington to be with his daughter.

He was on the next train out, and arrived to see all the newspaper men in force hanging out by the jail with their pads and pens out, trying to gain an insight into more of the developing story. They did not know who Big Ish was just yet, so he was safe for the moment. But by the time he had visited with his only daughter, they had been informed of the big man's purpose for being in their city.

As he exited the jail where his Mary Agnes was being detained, he tried to avoid the men desperately seeking answers. He spoke not a word to one of them, and hurried on his way to find lodging, while he figured out what to do next.

Grace was there as well with Amos, but this time Ish did not hold his tongue.

"Grace, I know you are here for her, as well as he is being here for her, but I can only promise you that if he gets in my way, it will not end pretty for him," he told her.

Grace knew Amos was also one to never back down, but she also knew her former husband was right. As much as she despised the man, she knew when to back off. So, she asked Amos to head on back home until the trial could be set. She and Ish would work on the details, and she would let him know if she needed his assistance any further. She promised him that.

Amos was not happy at all, and swore he was there to ensure Mary Agnes had the things her father could not and had not provided. He was frustrated with Grace for even suggesting such a thing, and partially embarrassed that he would need to head back home without them both. This was not going to be easy for him, and he cursed Grace about in a stern, aggressive manner, letting her know of his frustration.

Grace was used to this by now. There was very little one could say that would deter her from what it was she knew was right in her heart. For she, too, was more afraid of what would become of her child, than she was of what a man could do to her in anger. She had seen and experienced enough for two lifetimes already, so these men would just need to put their differences aside and grow up, she thought to herself.

So, Amos headed back to the steel mill, and worked to keep his mind off what was transpiring in Wilmington. It was best if he stayed busy and kept his mind off of things that he had little to no control over.

The story by now had traveled home, and the men he worked with had all heard about his stepdaughter. Even though these men were as tough as the steel they handled, they knew better than to judge Mary Agnes, or to even bring it up in conversation. It was bad enough to face the wrath of Amos if he heard any different, but if Ish had found out, the men genuinely feared for their very lives.

There would be, and could be, no stopping the anger of a father who would do anything to protect the name and reputation of his children, no matter what they had done or were accused of doing. A father was there to protect them physically as well as their honor, and the men knew he would do both and well.

Chapter 7

* * *

Richard Howard had been born and raised in Portsmouth, Virginia in 1857. By the time he was arrested, he was a man aged to 37 years old, about to turn 38, and the accusations of him sleeping with a soon-to-be 15-year-old child were serious charges that could impact the rest of his life.

He would need to explain to his wife, Ida, and their children, what and why things had happened as they had. He was, in his own mind, trying to prove the case that the town of Wilmington was troubled by illegal activities that were growing out of control, and he felt entirely justified in the way he did this. The issue was, just how far did he go to prove his case?

The prosecution had a lot to sort through in order to prove their case, including whether Mary Agnes, or Trixy as she was referred to for the purpose of prostitution, had informed Mr. Howard of her true age. She was born December 31, 1880, so by the time the trial rolled around, she was not even 15 years of age.

They next had to prove that he was in the house in question several times and know the dates of those visits so they could prove that he in fact, was in the area when the suspected crimes had taken place. This was a huge one for the prosecution, as Richard had traveled out of the area a few times over the last few months to go back home.

The police would be used as witnesses, but the trouble with that was the fact Mary Agnes had somehow eluded arrest the first time around, even before the warrants were issued and before the arrests were made at the home where she was temporarily residing. Had she been tipped off by authorities, or perhaps, Richard G Howard himself, so that she would not be arrested and he would not need to stand trial?

There was a lot of work to do in a short period of time and they had one shot at this, or the case would be tossed out and Richard would be set free to resume life as he knew it.

Ishmael wrote to his sister, Theresa Heald Mills, to come down for the trial and help prove Mary Agnes' age for the courts. He also realized he needed someone close by that he trusted to keep him company, as this trial was starting to get the better of him, and he was surely worried about the outcome and what that would mean for his child, as she very much still was one.

As the case was being presented, only the police, the witnesses, their families, and some select newspaper folks were allowed to be present in the courtroom. This was a high-profile case that involved potential corruption throughout the legal system both in and around Wilmington, and now, the religious one as well. A young woman had potentially been abused by a much older adult, albeit with her full consent, but someone would still need to answer for the crimes, the missteps, and the allegations as they were.

Mary Agnes was the first witness to take the stand, and the opposing council did not hold back. They peppered her with questions to try and discount her as a reliable witness. She told them her age of not yet 15, and then told them she had told Mr. Howard that she was 19 on one occasion, and then 22 on another. When asked why, she shrugged and said she thought if she did not, she would get into some type of trouble as she knew he was well connected.

The attorney questioning her did not stop at that answer.

"Why did you feel you would get into trouble? Was it perhaps due to the nature of your activities? Were you not aware that prostitution was an illegal activity at any age? How about the alcohol that was being served in the house you lived in? Surely you knew that was a practice of the house, and that it was illegal to serve without a proper license, correct Ms. Heald?"

Although Mary Agnes was well spoken and carried herself well for a girl her age, she was starting to feel pressured from the questions being asked. She could not remember the exact dates Richard had visited with her, and nor could she remember what he drank and who exactly served him those drinks. She was starting to feel scared, and all her mother and father could do was sit and watch.

Ish felt the blood boiling throughout his body and wanted to rise and grab this man screaming questions towards his daughter, but thankfully for him, his sister was there to grab ahold of his arm, and keep him from going to jail.

It was hard to watch, and harder to imagine how this tiny girl whom he watched grow from a distance could have been mixed up in such an ordeal. He blamed himself for not being more present as she grew, but he was only trying to provide a better way of life. At least that was what he believed in his mind, anyways.

Grace was troubled as well, knowing she had somehow let her child slip out of her hands, and into this world she swore to keep her from. She had tried so hard to keep her safe in the town they lived in, that she forgot there was an entire world out there to find trouble in for anyone not aware.

Their son was very different. He had stayed back with his Uncle William, and although he knew the rumors to be true, he refused to acknowledge that his dear sister had done anything wrong. He looked at her like the big sister he had grown to adore, and nothing was going to change that for him. Nothing.

"So, you remember the date as between June 18 and June 24th, is that correct?" the attorney asked.

"Yes, somewhere in between those dates, yes," Mary Agnes responded.

"If you had to pin a date, which was it closer to? The

June 18 or the June 24?" She was asked.

Mary Agnes sat still for a moment as she tried to think. Clearly she was feeling the pressure to answer this question as accurately as possible, but she could not recall for certain. She knew, however, that this attorney was not going to accept a range of dates for something he considered so serious. So, she gave what she thought was the right answer.

"I would say closer to the June 18th date," she replied.

As this date was now used as a mark for the man questioning her, he began to trick her into focusing on that date particularly. From there, he asked her what her morning was like, and what time she thought she had met Mr. Howard on June 18th. This was important to him as it would help prove an alibi for his client, but Mary Agnes was truthfully being tricked into answering for a date that she was certainly unsure of.

As she left the stand, she looked over to where her parents were seated, embarrassed and hoping for some type of understanding and forgiveness that she knew would be hard to see in their faces.

Ish was stoned-faced, perhaps to keep himself from growing emotional throughout this trial. He knew he was going to be questioned about his daughter's age by her representing attorney, and he knew if he could not control his emotions, things could go from bad to worse in the blink of an eye.

When he took the stand, he explained that she was in fact, born December 31, 1880, and that she was born out of wedlock. Her parents had not decided to marry until after she was born. Then, he explained that they had one more child, and had divorced shortly after.

As he was answering questions, he was examining the life he had lived up to this point, and deep inside he was struggling with how things had gone. He was not where he expected to be, despite all the hard work he had put in. the countless hours as a puddler, and the traveling he had done for better wages that ultimately cost him his own leg.

Ish was a proud man, but in those moments, he was a lost tramp.

As he finished answering the questions asked of him, he could be seen with his head hanging low, walking back to where his sister was, and sulking over this entire charade of a trial.

Richard and his brother were in the courtroom of course, as well as another man by the name of Henry Ferrier.

Mr. Ferrier was another of the so-called private detectives who was arrested alongside Richard but seemed to be a scapegoat for the movement.

The attorney for Richard homed in on the June 18 date, asking where he was at that exact date and time.

"Why I was back in Portsmouth, Va with my lovely wife, Ida, and our beautiful children. I had headed back before the 18th and did not return to this city until very late on the 19th," he answered.

"So tell me, sir. Who, if anyone, was with you that could attest to the same?" asked the attorney.

Richard answered with a calm collectiveness as if he had nothing to hide. He seemed to be an honest witness who had all his answers ready to go with not a second of hesitation. It turns out, at least by way of his answers, that he had his brother, the Dr. Reverend John H. Howard, Reverend John T. Bozman, and Professor Charles Sturtevant with him on his return trip home.

His witnesses were respected, professional members of the community, and appeared to be just as calm and collected as Richard had been during questioning.

After a short break, the judge returned to the room and, upon hearing and believing the alibi presented by Richard Howard, dismissed all charges just like that.

Mary Agnes was free to go, but no charges were going to stick to Richard for whatever it may have been he had done wrong. He thanked his attorney, and began to walk out of the courtroom, first turning towards Mary Agnes with a smile, and then catching the eye of her father, Big Ish. His smile quickly disappeared, and he hurried himself past the doors and exited the building, knowing that he did not want to grab this man's attention any more than he had already done.

As the summer went on, further charges would be brought against the house Mary Agnes stayed in, and now, Henry Ferrier.

Henry felt abandoned by the movement and the people that swore to protect him, and was ashamed of what he had done. He came truthfully to the courts, and swore that

Richard had knowingly had an affair with young Mary Agnes, even if he did not truly know her real age.

But it did not matter at that point. He was now fighting for his own freedom, very much alone, and perhaps that is why the judge took mercy on him. Charges were dismissed, and the case was dropped from any further hearings.

But the damage was done, and Mary Agnes was on her way to a troubled life, only she had no idea of how troubled it would become.

Chapter 8

* * *

Ishmael headed back to Lancaster City to start work again, and asked Mary Agnes to watch out for her while he could not. He tried to make her feel like what had happened was nothing more than a part of her past so that she could move on from it, but he was not certain himself. All he could do was hope that she learned a valuable lesson from all the trauma she experienced both before and during the court proceedings.

But he also started to look at himself from a different perspective. Maybe it was time for him to slow down some from the brutal days of steel working and focus on getting his affairs in order so that he could be a more present father. Maybe he should get back home more than not, and watch his kids grow, before it was too late to watch. If he could find work back home and steer clear of trouble, just maybe he could make it all make sense.

He lost his mother and his aging father was not getting any younger. Ish loved his family, despite his clear absence, but he knew he needed to do much more to show that to them.

He managed to stay out of trouble for most of the next few years, which for him was unheard of. Although there were the occasional scraps to be had, and those were important at times in his eyes to prove his worth and to stand his ground, he found a way to stay out of jail.

His brother, William, raised his family in a way that Ish admired greatly. He was always present, loved his wife like no man he had seen before, and worked hard at the plant to provide. Still, though, William told Ish he felt he had a different calling. A calling where he could make a true difference in the town he loved and assist the people whom he felt needed it.

While the two men did not know what that would be, they talked about it often enough that Big Ish wanted that for his brother. He figured that at least one of them should follow their dreams and accomplish something along the journey.

In the cold winter of January 1898, Ish was sent a message from his big brother back home in Conshohocken, that their sister Theresa, had passed. Her husband had died a few years prior to her, leaving it so that her two sons, John Aurthur Mills and William Mills were now left with no parents to care for them. It would be an orphanage for them both if someone didn't step up and quickly.

William talked it over with his wife Mary, both deciding that they could add just one more small mouth to feed, and decided on William, who was just 4 years old. John, who had turned 9, was sent to live at the St. Johns Orphan

Asylum in the city of Philadelphia, as the family thought it best and there were really no other options.

There was no way Ish was in any condition to care for another child, when he had trouble being home for his own two that called him father, and to ask Grace to see to a child not of her blood, seemed unfair and a little selfish. Besides, there was a lot of rumbling on the street that Amos was becoming more difficult to calm down and causing arguments and fist fights wherever he walked.

In May of that same year, Mary Agnes was back living in Conshohocken with her mother Grace, and her stepfather, Amos. She was trying to get things back in order but struggling with the fact most men found her extremely desirable and she craved that attention.

One such man was constable John Redmond, of the fourth ward. On May 21st, a crisp Saturday evening, John and Mary Agnes were walking home from an afternoon together, when Grace spotted them. She immediately summoned Amos, who was with a drink inside the home, and told him how displeased she was with the sight of the two together.

Amos swung open the door and saw the young constable approaching, and immediately a vicious argument ensued, causing both men to shout profanities at one another, while Grace hurried her daughter away from the noise and what was to surely come.

Amos Alexander produced an axe he had been wielding, and without a single moment of hesitation, slammed it into the head of John.

Somehow John was able to stumble backwards enough to escape the brutal fight and summon Justice Heywood, who quickly issued a warrant for the arrest of his attacker. Both John and another constable by the name of Thomas Clark, returned to serve the warrant onto Amos, but proceeded with extreme caution, knowing the man they were about to arrest.

Smartly, John decided to stand back from his partner, as Thomas then knocked on the front door to the home of Amos and Grace. In about a minute or so, Amos showed back up to the front door, opened it, aggressively pushing past Thomas, and marched headfirst towards John once again, with that axe still in hand.

Another two or three blows were thrown but Redmond somehow eluded them all. But on the very next one, he caught Redmond once again on the top of his head, knocking him down and unconscious. Amos stood there, with no remorse on his darkened face, as if he had simply killed a rabbit for dinner.

Mary Agnes was inside screaming as her mother Grace tried desperately to shield her from the violence taking place out front of their home. She did not need her to see the guy she had just spent the afternoon with, laying in a pool of his own blood pouring from his head, by the hands of the man who swore he loved her like a daughter.

Clark hurried himself past the two men, as Amos was now retreating to the comforts of his home. He was able to get some further assistance to help take young John to the station house to assess his injuries. It was first thought that the young man was in danger of dying that night, but thankfully for John, he would make a full recovery.

The burgess issued a second warrant for Amos Alexander, and this time, Captain Courduff, a well-known and no-nonsense gentleman, was sent to arrange the arrest. After considerable struggle and another altercation with Amos acting as a wild man does, he was brought under enough control, arrested, and sent to jail for a hearing to determine his penalty.

In a turn of events, Amos decided to also press charges on Redmond for assault, and forcibly detaining Mary Agnes, as initially, as Amos put it, he would not let her go into the arms of her mother.

To the shock of many, once again, Amos was let go with a stern warning to settle down and stop his foolishness and raging ways or the next time could be it for him.

Mary Agnes began to confide in her mother that Amos was seemingly more and more jealous of everything she was doing. Any time she mentioned a boy, he would quickly fire off questions about his name and where he lived and why she was interested in him in the first place. At first she thought that maybe it was just as a parent did, and after having the trouble she did in Wilmington, she could understand some overprotectiveness. But as time went on, it just seemed to grow more and more odd, as his questioning and jealousy seemed more bizarre and out of place.

Grace had noticed too, but she was more optimistic that

he was just being overly protective. She reminded Mary Agnes that he had basically raised her in the absence of Ishmael, and only saw her as a strong, caring father would.

Mary Agnes thought to ask her father for advice, but she knew what would happen if she did. Big Ish would ask questions only as he was simultaneously trying to pummel Amos into next week. She did not want him to get into any further trouble, as he has seemed to be on a much better path over the last few years. So, she decided to just stay quiet and hope that this would pass, and Amos would simply let her be.

That same year, towards the end of the summer, Amos had been drinking early in the day, and for reasons known only to him, headed over to where Grace's former father-in-law, Old Ish, lived, with Grace just a step behind. There were rumors that the elder Ish had gotten wind of the growing anger Amos was showcasing towards others, including his granddaughter Mary Agnes, and his grandson, William. Ish, although sixty-two years of age and in failing health, was still a tough old steelworker himself.

But even though he meant well, he was much too old for the stronger and younger Amos, who tried to break down the front door to the home on Oak Street that Ish owned and lived in for years. When he could not open the front door, he decided to try his luck on the rear one, stumbling around the house and over to where it was located. Grace was still within walking distance, seemingly on board with what Amos had set out to do.

Once there, with a single kick, he was able to break the rear door open, and began screaming for the "old man" to come out and face him like a gentleman.

"You old son of a bitch, I'll kill you," he began to scream.

A man named Frank Huzzard, who was a friend of Old Ish, was present in the home at the time and tried to reason with Amos to leave the old man be.

"If I get a crack at old Ishmael, I'll lay him out," Amos continued.

At that moment, old Ish had heard enough. This was his house he worked hard for, and tough or not, Amos was not going to scare him off. He walked as quickly as he could over to where Amos was screaming and told him,

"Well, here I am, do as you say."

Amos, who had a fence pail with him in hand, swung it at Ish's head, clobbering the old man and sending him to the floor below in a great deal of apparent pain. As the blood leaked from his head, Frank ran out past the duo, and tried to find help for his overmatched friend.

By the time the constables arrived at the Heald house, Amos and Grace were nowhere to be found.

A warrant was issued once again for this man of short temperament, and because of the nature of the injury to the elder Ish, it was time for some severe punishment, and Amos knew it would come this time around.

As they headed home, Amos told Grace,

"This will be the last of my freedom for some time to come, I feel it."

When they were finally able to apprehend Amos, again not without a great struggle ensuing, he was sobered up enough and would say little to nothing at first. He was brought to the jail he began to know so well, to await trial, and a $500.00 bond was set. He would not be able to come up with that type of money, so he sat cold until the morning of the hearing a few weeks later.

Many of the residents who lived on "Stone Row," showed up in support of Old Ish. He was well liked in the neighborhood and bothered no one. If you needed something, and he could provide it, he damn sure would have. That was just the type of man he was raised to be, and always remained.

At the hearing, Amos testified that he was indeed drunk, but that it was not he who struck the old man. He claimed that Frank Huzzard, in an attempt to remove Amos from the home, had swung the pail at him, and he simply ducked out of the way, allowing for the pail to sadly hit Ish. He further testified that Frank had in fact grabbed him, and swung the big Amos around, kicking him from the back steps, down to the rear yard grounds and onto his hands and knees.

After he finished telling his version and the other folks at the hearing testified to what they saw happen, the judge handed down his ruling without a moment of hesitation and no time off the stand needed.

"Amos Alexander, I sentence you to prison for the term of no less than nine months for your actions upon Ishmael Heald."

And that was that.

Now the only fear was, what would Big Ish do when he arrived back in town to see his family? Mary Agnes was at least happy about the fact that Amos was locked away and would give her a break from the jealous rampage, and also to where her father could not get to him once he was made aware of the news.

As tough and angry as she knew Amos was, she knew no man she had ever encountered could fend off the likes of her father, Big Ish, especially not when you messed around with his family and loved ones. It was as if Amos had signed a death warrant that was just waiting to be properly served.

Now, Amos had to wonder with nine months away to think about it, would Big Ish seek his revenge and if so, how would he handle the big fella?

Chapter 9

* * *

William had had enough of the way the men and women of Conshohocken were acting in lawlessness and foolishness, and decided it was time for him to leave the steel mill years behind and go to what he felt was calling him, a way to make change, and to do it with a badge backing him.

Conshohocken decided to elect a police force, and William felt an immediate calling to run. He was well liked, intelligent, a strong family man that people could clearly see, and came from tough stock that went back generations in this country. But he was also known as a fair man, and well spoken. He understood that people had their quarrels, but that not everyone meant harm. For those that did intend harm to come from their actions, he wanted to set an example that things were going to change for the good of the people of Conshohocken, if he had anything to do with it.

With Amos behind bars still, things were incredibly difficult for Grace and the two kids. So Mary Agnes decided to head to the city of Philadelphia with a friend, and Grace knew what that meant. But she also knew what sort of say did she really have in the matter and who would help her stop Mary Anges from doing as she wished?

Grace was struggling and living wherever she could find a place to lay her head. Her son, William, was bonding more with his father, Ish, and learning the ways of the world through his eyes. But Ish was not teaching his young son how to fight. He was showing how to not fight. He, of course, wanted young William to be able to defend himself, but what Ish wanted for his son more than anything was to learn to not live as he had. If that was the lesson all his pain and struggles taught his son, so be it.

For now, though, they were surviving more than living, and Grace felt as though she was failing those that relied on her for support and comfort. Why did Amos need to be so difficult and headstrong all the time? His temper was growing increasingly short over the past few years, and she wondered if she had made another bad decision in marrying a second man who could not keep himself out of jail.

By this point, Ish was still doing well and avoiding most of the trouble others were finding. He had put in the back of his mind what Amos had done to his aging father, but he promised himself he would never let that go entirely. If he ever crossed paths with Amos Alexander again, there would be retribution, jail or no jail. There would be no talking him out of that.

William was settling into his new career, and learning the

law as best he could from both the books he was reading and those other officers around him. The people in town either respected him for taking such an important role in a mostly lawless town or resented him for what they believed was an act of betrayal for wearing the badge.

Either way, though, William was excited for what was to come, and his father, although in increasingly failing health, was proud of his eldest son. His first born had gone through life avoiding the troubles that Conshohocken, and really, the world, presented to him daily. He understood that there were times you could not avoid the fighting and illegal ways, especially with the men in the steel mills forming gangs that swore,

"This here be our neighborhood boy. You go around this street we own, not through, or you be picking up your teeth from the ground below."

William had learned to keep his head down when he needed, and up when that was going to get his point across. He was smart when it came to the streets and could some-how get through just about any area of Conshohocken with little to complain about. He was respected by the tough men of Conshohocken for being honest, fair, and a gentleman who didn't go looking to prove himself to other men. Plus, he was a good family man, so he avoided the troubles that came from eyeing a woman whom someone else claimed as their gal, which seemed to start most of the fights in town.

His younger brother, Ish, may not have understood why

William chose that side of the law, but he, too, respected his brother for the decision. It was just that Ish had a different perspective on those who he claimed tried hiding behind a piece of neatly shaped metal that meant nothing, no how, to him.

With Mary Agnes in the City of Philadelphia, Grace was forced to make some decisions when Amos was finally released after his nine months away. Could she stay, or should she stay, with a man whom she felt was growing more attached and protective of her own daughter? And was there a reason Mary Agnes was feeling more uncomfortable lately with how he spoke to her, especially after he had a few drinks in him? She knew Ish was already pissed off about the fence pail incident with Old Ish and was out for blood, but if that man knew about what Mary Agnes was worried about, surely he would kill Amos without hesitation. Although Grace did not like Big Ish, she did not want him behind bars for life. That would do no good for the children, even though they were not so small anymore.

In 1899, life was going on as it did, and Amos was more than halfway through his sentence for beating that Old Ish senseless. He had not had a single drop of the drink in months, and he, too, felt as if he made some bad decisions in life, but regret was not on the front of his mind. He was still an angry, bitter man, and felt that everything he had done for Grace and those two kids went largely unnoticed.

As for his thoughts on Big Ish, well, he knew there may come a time when the two strong men would cross paths, and he wondered if he could take the big man or not. No one had ever heard of a single man handling Ish in all the years they had known of him. In fact, it seemed men, women, and even the law would not have a decent chance, with both legs or not.

But Amos had never lost a battle either, for those men in the steel town from neighboring streets knew of him and his reputation as well, and they knew if they battled with Amos, they, too, were in for a rough night that would more than likely end with a visit to the local hospital.

Amos had a lot of time to wonder what he would need to do when he got out. He felt betrayed, even though Grace had defended his actions in court, and lied to the judge about what had happened. She knew that if he went to jail, she would be out on the streets and once again very alone. She could not ask for help from the Heald family, because she had defended her husband over the truth, and they would not allow her any help with her lies against their name.

By July, he would have his freedom back and would need to find a new place to live. But first, he needed to gain his freedom, and convince Grace and Mary Agnes that he was a different man from the one they saw hauled away and locked up. He had not touched a drop of the devil's poison and felt that it showed a different side of him that they could surely be proud of.

But he also had lost his position at the mill and would need to secure some new type of work and quickly, so that he could pay the bills and put a roof over their heads once again. He was not made aware yet that Mary Agnes had left Conshohocken for the city, nor did he know if Grace was going to give him another chance at their marriage.

Mary Agnes, for her part, had left what happened in Wilmington drift off to the deep past. She never heard from Richard Howard again, and nor did she ever expect to. He had been let off the hook and moved back down to Portsmouth to live his life out with his family. Right or wrong, she no longer cared to revisit a dead horse.

She wanted the comforts of a big city and appreciated the attention the boys and men with the most money provided to her. It felt good, having grown up in such a poor and filthy lifestyle, to have others spending money just to spend time with you or buying you lavish gifts, even if it wasn't in the best of ways. She figured it was temporary, and she could save enough money to get her and her mother into a much more suitable environment. She told herself over and over,

"This is just temporary."

Nine months had passed, and there, on the streets of the old neighborhood, stood Amos Alexander, trying to figure out where Grace had gone. She did not visit him one time, and he had no idea if she had read, or even received, the letters he wrote to her. She never replied if she had.

But he still figured if she had not found a new man to support her, he still had a chance at redemption. So he asked around if anyone had seen his Grace. Most people didn't want to be bothered, but he was relentlessly pursuing, and had a rough way of getting what he wanted.

The neighbors needed no trouble from him, so eventually, one of the men told Amos a rumor of where he had heard she was staying. Amos never thanked the man, as it was just not his way. Instead, he turned away, and headed to where he was told she may be.

When he arrived, he realized that it was a relative of Grace's, and quickly knocked on the door. The woman who answered the door looked shocked at first and told him that if she wanted him to know where she was staying, she would let him know herself. Amos started to shout at the woman, but she was not like others he could intimidate. She stopped Amos mid-sentence and asked him,

"What's the matter with you? Ya deaf as a fool?"

Just then, Grace came around the corner on her way back from cleaning a house and saw Amos standing there. It was the first time in nine months that she had seen her husband, and when he saw her, he smiled and told her,

"Baby, I'm home. Let's get back to things, but better. What do you say, deal?"

Chapter 10

* * *

By mid-July of 1899, the town was under a heat wave, and Amos was struggling to find work that he had done so easily in the past. Neither of which was good for his short temperament.

Grace felt that nothing was going to change, so she wrote her daughter in Philadelphia a letter to see how things were in the city. Maybe there was something for her there where her daughter was living for the summer.

Mary Agnes was so very pleased to hear from her mother, but knew it was desperation that led her to put pen to that paper, and even just reading her words, she could hear the pain through both the simple words her mother wrote and the frantic manner they seemed to be scribbled in and knew she needed help quickly.

So, she invited both her and Amos to come to the city and told her she had plenty of contacts that could help secure work for Amos, and even help Grace find a house-keeping position. Plus, at just eighteen years of age, Mary

Agnes was making enough money plying her trade that she would be able to help both of them more than she ever had before. With the promise of help, both Amos and Grace agreed to move down to the brick lined road of Wood St and settled in to number 407.

They removed the few items they had to their names, and headed towards the city to see where Mary Agnes was thriving. On the way, Amos seemed off. He was not talking as much as he had immediately following his release from prison, and seemed to be bothered by something. Grace figured that maybe it was just taking Amos a bit more to get used to being on the outside after having been locked away for the better part of a year. Plus, as a proud man, it could be the help Mary Agnes extended that made him feel less of a man.

Whatever it was, he wasn't as excited to get out of the area as Grace seemed to be. She was happy to be getting a new fresh start in a different city, and to be able to be closer to her only daughter. Her son, William, had been spending more time with his father in Lancaster, and seemed to remove himself from her life, based on the fact she would not leave Amos. William did not like him much at all, and felt he was going to end up really hurting someone, most likely Grace, if they did not get far away from this man and his antics.

But Grace was struggling, had little money to her name, and felt as if she was in a terrible predicament for a woman of those times, and therefore, had few options outside of staying with him.

William also did not approve of his sister's way of life, as he was a straight arrow, a hard-working man who went in to work early in the morning, came home late in the evening, and kept mostly to himself. That was what he figured was the best way to accomplish what one wanted, or needed, in life.

When William told his father about the move they all had made, Ish sat back in his chair, took a swig of his drink, and stared out into the summer evening sky. The sounds of crickets were covered by the laughing of tough men who worked the furnaces, and who would be drinking late into the evening.

"Well, William. I don't know what to think of this all. I tried to protect your sister, but she has her own ways of this world, and how is a guy to straighten her out when she won't listen none at all?" Ish asked.

William did not have an answer. He was sorely worried about his older sister, but he did not know the extent of the dangers she was about to face. For him, it was more the fact that she was a beautiful, young, intelligent woman whom he thought could do just about anything she desired, and here she was, selling herself to men who ought to know better. It did not sit well with young William at all.

"You think you will ever run into Amos? What will you do, for what he did to granddad?" William asked.

Ish didn't say much of anything. He wanted to tell his son that he would rip his arms from their sockets and beat him senseless over his thick head as he had beat his father with that pail, but what good would that do? He would end up back in jail, and what then? Where would William go to live? He had not wanted to stay with his mother because of this other man, so all Ish would accomplish would be to cause trouble for the lot of them.

So, Ish kept that to himself, although in his own mind, he knew the answer. If he had a genuine crack at Amos, he would probably take his shot, and deal with the consequences afterwards as he had often done throughout his life already. He knew that even with the greatest of intentions, his rage would find a way to escape his more reasonable thoughts and destroy what it needed to.

His brother, William, had told Ish,

"Brother, listen here. Let that man find his own demise. Believe me, I want that man put away for the rest of his life for the thing he did to dad, but going and hurting him, as much as we would want to, will do little good for us. Let the law and the laws of God handle that nonsense. Believe me, Ish. What God has in store for him, will be far worse than either of us could ever do to that man."

While Ish did not care much for the law, he trusted his brother and knew, as hard as it was to listen, that he was more than likely right. William was a smart man, and a Godly man. He went to church on Sundays and volunteered wherever he could help. He knew things about the God that created them more than Ish knew, so if he said let God handle it, then who was he to argue?

As for Mary Agnes, Ish was frustrated and worried, but

little could be done about that. He blamed himself for not being around as he should have been all those years. He blamed Grace for letting her do as she wished in the first place, and not being stronger for her daughter. And he blamed that town for being as rough and hard as it was and making her find a way out through any means she could.

Mary Agnes was having a grand time in the city, and she helped set up her mother and Amos in a small house they rented, with her help of course, and visited often. She would stop over daily, mostly when Amos was supposedly out looking for work, and sit and have tea with her mother.

Grace was struggling with wanting to feel proud of her girl, and wanting to remove her from the shame of this world she was tangled up in. It was tough, because what could she do? Her Mary Agnes provided not only a life for herself, but for Grace and Amos, as they could not seem to catch a break and desperately needed her help. If it weren't for her money she made from those boys and men with that high class money to spend, they would surely be on the streets by now.

"How's William doing, mom? Have you heard much from him?" Mary Agnes asked curiously.

Grace took a sip from her teacup and opened up to her daughter,

"He's. Well, he ain't happy with me now. That damn father of yours has him thinking he's better off with him and not me. I raised ya both by myself when he was off doing God knows what. And now? Where did that all get me?" Grace replied.

Mary Agnes missed her brother, but she understood that sometimes a boy needed his father, and that was just how boys were at his age. It wasn't personal, she didn't feel, but more that it was time for him to become a man, and who better to teach him than the lad's father? Plus, she knew William and Amos did not see eye to eye, and with Amos being away for the past nine months, who was going to be a better example for him?

"Mom, you know that he just wants to see if he can build a relationship with his father, as boys often do. He needed to get out, just as I did. That has nothing to do with you, and everything to do with us growing up. We are setting our wings, and readying them to fly away," Mary Agnes replied.

She was right, and Grace understood that, but for all the hardships Grace had experienced in this life, dating all the way back to losing her own father and brothers in those treacherous waters off the coast of Tory Island, Ireland, she had always thought her children would just be there every time she needed them to be. She was not ready for them to fly from the nest, as they were beginning to do. What mother was?

Grace was excited for the prospect that Mary Agnes had saved enough money to get her own place, away from the speakeasies and the perverted men who visited them, and find a decent fella who worked hard, made decent money of his own, and would provide her with grandchildren she was truly looking forward to. Grace was a radiant beauty, glowing as most women could not imagine even in their wildest dreams. Her skin was perfect, and her flowing dark hair reminded Grace of a queen in olden times. Mary Agnes was considered one of the prettiest women of her time, and because of that, Grace just knew good things were in store for her child.

Amos arrived back at the home as the two were cleaning up from chatting over tea.

"Oh, Mary Agnes, it's good to see you," Amos said.

She smiled at him, a cautious smile, as she had spoken to him so little since he was released from prison. She knew he was having trouble adjusting, and blamed everyone around him for the time he had spent away. So she wanted to tread carefully as not to upset him in any way, including any mentioning of her grandfather, whom Amos had beaten.

As she said her goodbyes, she asked her mother if it would be alright for her to take her shopping later that week. Of course, Grace would agree, but Amos seemed to take that personally, as if this young girl was able to provide where he could not, and perhaps she was rubbing it into his face. She surely only had good intentions for her mother, though. She was making money and had plenty extra with which to make her mother feel like a real woman, and that was all she wanted for her.

They agreed to meet again on Tuesday, July 25th, 1899.

Mary Agnes would take her mother out for a few things, and when Amos would arrive home, they would have dinner together, and then she would be on her way to her own home, which was just a short distance from where both Amos and Grace were living now.

That Tuesday came, and Mary Agnes started her short walk over to pick up her mother, excited to be able to give her this gift. She was feeling especially proud that morning, as she smiled to herself and held her head high in the air as she walked down Fairmont Avenue, over to Fourth Street, and then onto Wood where they were meeting at Grace's place.

But the day would prove to be more than anyone could ever expect it to be, and lives were changed that evening forever, in the blink of an eye.

Chapter 11

* * *

The papers would call it a "mysterious death". The police, "a suicide for certain," they told the papers. No one knew for sure what had actually happened, and rumors swirled around towns for miles, as the world for the Heald family was most certainly changed forever.

It started out as intended. Mary Agnes picked her mother up at the house as they had planned, and took her out shopping at some of Philadelphia's grandest stores. They walked around, talked about mostly nothing of great importance, and ended up back home before the evening came calling, just in time for supper to be prepared.

Grace talked Mary Agnes into staying for supper and told her when the day's light closed, Amos would walk her as far as she needed him to, so she would not be alone at night. Mary Agnes hesitantly agreed but prepared the food for the evening alongside her mother.

Meanwhile, Ish was visiting Conshohocken with young William, intending on looking for a place to return to. He had wanted to come home to the town he was raised in and see if he could remove himself from the trouble he had so easily found out in Lancaster City. On top of that, his boy was missing the family they had back there and was feeling a bit homesick.

His brother was excited to see both Ish and his nephew for certain. It had been some time since the two of them sat down and chewed the fat. Ish looked better than he had in recent memory and didn't have his customary fresh cuts or deep blue bruises that William was accustomed to seeing on his brother.

They laughed and shared stories of how life was for each of them over the past few years or so. Willliam talking of tales from the streets of arresting young men for stealing chickens in broad-day-light, no less, and Ish telling of young William working with him while cussing men looked on with just enough respect to make Ish proud.

Life seemed simple and both men, seemed genuinely happy with where they stood for a change.

When Willam, Ish's brother, was contacted that July morning, he was as white as a ghost. There was no way he heard the news correctly. It was virtually impossible, so the only logical answer was that someone had made a terrible error in identifying the deceased soul. In fact, he had hoped it was just some stupid, cruel joke someone was playing.

He walked back home to where his brother was staying while on his return trip, and upon entering the house, took his hat off, sat down in a chair just inside the entrance of the home, and looked down to the pine floors beneath his shoes.

Ish was in the back of the house, getting himself another coffee, before heading out to see his father that morning. When he walked in and saw William back so soon after leaving earlier that morning, he knew something wasn't right.

"What is it? William, what is it?" Ish asked with great concern.

He knew by the way his brother had sat there stone-faced and pale as anything, that it wasn't anything easy. This was dealing his older brother a blow as he had never seen before. Was it their father? Did something happen to one of the other officers on duty while he was at work? The town was rough from east to west and north to south, so anything was possible.

"It…," William began, before a long, worrisome pause.

"William, just tell me. What happened?" Ish asked again, this time with a voice of concern wondering if he truly was ready for the answer.

William looked up to Big Ish, stared his brother in the eyes, and just shot it out of his lips.

"Mary Agnes was found in Philadelphia, laying on the ground unconscious."

Ish's eyes opened wide, wondering how bad it was. Why was she found unconscious and where was she. He would need to find a way to the city as quickly as he could and see his little girl. But William continued before Ish could get a word in.

"She's dead, Ish. She passed away late last night."

Ishmael was now the one stoned-faced, and understandably quiet for a man who wore his large heart on his sleeve without a care from what others may think. He was built different from most men, and one could tell when he was about to cause trouble, right before he did. But this time, William wasn't sure what he was seeing in his brother's face.

Ish eventually dropped his eyes down, went back to the rear of the house, out the back door, and sat on the steps. He needed a moment to himself, and for the first time in his life, he did not know what he intended to do, or for that matter, needed to do. His one and only daughter had died last night, while he enjoyed a keg of beer with his brother and sang songs, laughing and enjoying the evening away. She was lying there dead and helpless when he was just a few towns away, and unaware of her life being pulled from her body.

William came out after a few moments and touched his brother on the shoulder.

"Brother let's get you to the city and see what we can find out. I wasn't told much more than what I just told you, so let's figure out what happened. I won't leave you. I promise," William said.

Ish knew he had to get to the city, but truthfully, his one good leg and one bad leg did not want to move. He was frozen in place and struggling to gain a will to do much of anything. But after a few more minutes and more urging from his brother, he got up, wiped his eyes, and walked back into the house to gather his stuff. He would need his brother with him for several reasons, but mostly, to just be there by his side.

They left almost immediately and headed for Philadelphia by way of train, and once arriving, headed towards the hospital she was brought to. Ish knew he was about to see his Mary Agnes for the first time ever when she could not tell him she loved him with that big, beautiful smile of hers, and that hurt him deeply. He would be unable to hold her close and remind her that if she ever needed him, he would be there just as quickly as he could. But last night, he had not been there when she needed him the most.

Minutes felt like hours as he waited to see her, and William reminded him that if he saw Grace and Amos, he needed to do everything he could to stay as calm as could be, for Mary Agnes.

"Ish, you are no good behind bars if you do something that I know you feel the need to do. Just be here for the right reasons for now. Let it go as best you can. Please, at least for now," William said.

He knew his brother was struggling and could see his knuckles white as could be from squeezing his fist tightly. This was not a good sign, and although William was strong in his own right, he was not capable of pulling Ish off of any man when he got going at his worst. It put a fear in him, but he prayed to God that he gives his brother just a little relief and calm him down enough that he would not need to try.

Grace and Amos had left the hospital already and were

back at the station speaking to the officers about how they recalled the entire day and evening going. They were searching for any clues and possible reasons for this tragedy to make at least a little sense, but could find none.

Amos told the police that he and Mary Agnes started out along the same route she took each time she visited, and nothing seemed unusual to him. He talked with her about the shopping both she and Grace had done earlier in the day, and that she seemed delighted with it all. There was nothing to suggest she was depressed or angry in the least.

The police asked questions as he spoke. They wanted to know about the people around them. Were they alone on the walk? Did anyone else see them that could maybe shed some light on what may have happened? How about the house where she lived? Did she ever get there or did they, for any reason, stop short?

Amos was calm and answered each question as it was asked. He told them he intended to walk her just a short distance, when a young, handsomely dressed man with a hat and smart clothing stopped by to say hi to Mary Agnes. He whispered something to her, and Amos felt that she must have known him by the way they smiled at each other, so he stepped back and gave her some privacy.

The police asked if he had ever seen this man before, or if Mary Agnes mentioned him by name.

"I had not laid eyes on him in my life, and she spoke to him in private, so if she said his name, I surely did not hear it," Amos responded.

The police asked him to please continue.

"Well, as I was telling you, they seemed to know each other quite well. I studied the man so that I may let her mother know, in case she may know who the man was. He was, as I said, dressed well from head to toe. His complexion was light, and he wore a sandy moustache upon his face. The suit he wore was gray and on the top of his head, a brown colored fedora."

The police took notes of the description, figuring with this detailed of one, someone would come forward who knew this man and his business with young Mary Agnes that evening.

"So, as I said, I gave them space, and then excused myself by saying goodbye to Mary Agnes. I just never figured that it would be the last time I would see her alive," Amos finished with somewhat of a bewildered expression.

When Mary Agnes reached the boarding house, she was alone, as another boarder had told them. She came inside to grab something from her room, and then left. There was no sign she was in a panicked state, nor one that she was upset with anyone or anything. She was just as normal as she ever had been.

Shortly thereafter, she was found dying on the sidewalk of North Third street, between numbers 611 and 613. As of now, no witnesses had come forward with any information on the strange, well-dressed young man. He was not seen by another soul on those same streets they walked, and even though a few had seen Mary Agnes, no one saw her with anyone other than Amos. But she had arrived at the boarding house alone and left it alone. That much they were sure of.

The only witness to her death was a man who claimed to have seen her fall to the ground just before she passed. He quickly ran over to see what was wrong with the young, beautiful woman, only to see she was unconscious as could be, with her lips pressed tightly closed.

She was removed quickly to Hahnemann Hospital, where she was pronounced dead.

On examining her body and her clothing, no letters were found stating why she may have wanted to take her young life. When the police went to search her room that she had left prior to falling, they found no signs of anything that she was unhappy or having any signs of wanting to die. The only evidence to her death was found nearby where she collapsed. A single bottle of carbolic acid, with the label hastily removed in what seemed like an attempt to hide the name of the pharmacy it had originated from.

Grace was devastated. She knew there was no reason for her child to end her life. She demanded that the police find the man whom Amos saw with her and question him on why he had giving her that acid. Of course he would be the only one to know, as there wasn't another person from the time they left until she died, whom she was seen with. Other than Amos, who told the police all he knew.

The coroner was called in to do his own investigation, and decided, with only one morning of investigation, that the young lady, after having a few drinks, had taken the fatal draught in a spasm of remorse.

Grace spoke bluntly to the deputy coroner, saying,

"If any man performs any post-mortem examination on my child, I will stick a knife into the man who put the knife into her body."

The coroner was surprised by this and asked her what her reasoning behind this statement was.

Grace later told him that she was excited at the time and the horror of having the body of her only daughter mutilated caused her to say things for which she did not mean.

The physicians at the hospital later told both her and Ish as well as the police, that she had taken enough of the acid to kill six grown adults. After hearing this, the coroner decided there was no need for a post-mortem examination after all.

The police had no suspects, and therefore determined, along with the coroner and the physicians who attended to her when she arrived, that Mary Agnes Heald had decided to take her life. And so, the case was closed and no further investigation was ever needed.

The mysterious man whom Amos claimed to have seen before heading back home to Grace was never found, and life for Grace and Ishmael was shaken in the hardest, most brutal way possible. Their only girl was now dead.

Chapter 12

Both Grace and Ish had to return to their homes, painfully aware that their child, their only daughter, Mary Agnes, was no longer coming home to be with them.

It didn't seem real for either, and to make matters even worse, the newspapers had painted their child in a not so positive light, exploring the fact that she had been a high-end call girl for the well to do. The men and women of Conshohocken and the surrounding areas were shocked to learn about this once tiny, sweet, adorable girl who they fondly remembered laughing in the streets with friends or walking with her mother along the roads leading home, never without a fresh smile on her face.

For the police to have so hastily determined suicide, did not sit well with anyone, including the newspapers who reported the story. They wrote that something did not seem quite right, and that even after the police came to their decision, another investigation should be opened to find out who the stranger she spoke to was, and how on earth no one saw Mary Agnes from that point until she was found falling to the ground below while it was very much still light out.

But the second one was never opened. William made inquiries with the city's police department, but to no avail. He thought maybe they could do a little more digging and ask perhaps neighbors of the home she resided in, or even question the other women living in the home, if they could figure out who that last man was that Amos saw her with. Just one more clue or forgotten statement may make a big difference and crack the case, but he had to remind himself that he had a vested interest and no one else did.

But Ish was not so sure there was a mysterious man to begin with. He could not put his finger on why he felt this way, but he determined in his own heart that there may have never been such a fella on the streets, but why would Amos have fabricated such a person if it weren't true? What would be the point in doing so? That part, he did not know. To him, the man was a phantom made up by a man hiding a secret that only he knew.

And though he brought that to the attention of her mother, Grace, she was painfully struggling herself and lashed out, wanting to hear no more of that nonsense. In her mind, what Amos had told her was factual. And that would be that. Why would he lie about the girl he saw as a daughter and loved more than almost anything on earth?

Amos seemed to steer clear of others for a short time

after her death, especially that Big Ish. He knew that in losing his only daughter, Ish was better left alone to heal his wounds. The issue remained, though, that Ish had it out for Amos, ever since he mercilessly beat his father over the head with an old fence pail. But Old Ish reminded his son, winning battles does not mean you win the war. Focus on getting your life in order, and remember, you still have that boy who not only loves and respects you, but now more than ever, needs you. There will always be a time for revenge, but not always a time to do what is right. You don't often get second chances.

Besides, William now being a part of the law and in charge of keeping order in his town, was always keeping one eye out for Amos. All he needed to do was to catch that son-of-a-bitch stepping out of line one time, just one hair out of place and he would handle the rest. Amos felt as if his time in Conshohocken was nearing an end.

So he headed back to Norristown, and Grace, having little, decided to go back with him and hoped that he would settle down his ways and allow her to grieve in peace, and possibly giving her some support which she had truly never had from a man in her life. She just wanted someone to understand her and love her for all she was and had been through.

Ishmael headed back to Lancaster to retrieve his belongings as he, too, decided it was time to move back to the area and figure out what was to come next for him. He was a broken man, now both physically and mentally, and struggling to keep his mind off the damage his body wanted to cause. It was just how he was built, and he had fought against it for the past few years now, but that was going to end.

He started drinking once again, feeling as if he needed the liquor to cure his broken heart that seemed to be held together by nails and bandages. Life was not as he intended, nor was it looking as if it was ever going to go the way he had hoped.

His son, William, was quiet mostly about the death of his sister. He had not been close with her for a few years now, as both children sided with different parents, but he felt hurt for certain. He just grieved in a much different way. Seldom did he bring it up to anyone, and if you brought it to his attention, he quickly changed the subject before having to remember the past.

Grace was settling into her new place in Norristown and Amos was once again seeking employment so that he could pay the rent. He talked about Mary Agnes and her death, almost as if he were trying to convince Grace that that man was still out there and he was damn sure going to find him one of these days and set this straight. He could see him in his mind and would drop him with a heavy blow to the head the minute he saw him again, no questions asked. He swore to it.

"Amos, tell me. Tell me that you saw that man. That he was not a passerby stranger, and that he did as you had said he did. Was this man real?" Grace inquired with a sound of disbelief.

Amos tossed furniture upside down in their rental, screaming obscenities about the room, as he verbally slammed Grace for even questioning him,

"You think I pulled that fella out of thin air, do you now? As if I could describe him and his proper clothing right down to the shoes he wore so well from just my imagination. As if I were not her father as well, if not more than that waste of life, Ish. That what you are saying to me?"

Amos was steaming, and Grace just wanted to forget she ever asked him, but Amos was not one to forget. He stomped past her in a ferocious manner, having Grace fear for herself momentarily, and stormed out of the house off to God knows where, allowing the door to swing open and stay that way.

Grace wondered if she had asked that out of anger, sadness, or because maybe Ish was right about what he said. Maybe something didn't make much sense, but she quickly put those curious thoughts away, and decided that Mary Agnes was gone, and blaming others at this point was not going to bring her back. Although she had begged for justice, she also yearned for infinite peace. Not just for her though. Also, for her daughter, who now was outed to the world for the decisions she had made to support herself and gain a way out of the slums she was raised in.

Ish never had to hear anyone talk about her in his presence. He knew they were whispering, but no man had the nerve to state their opinions to him with any voice, so he was able to let that rest for now. His concern was to find a way to get life back to as normal as possible, and to ensure his boy, William, knew he was there for him.

The rest of the year would go by without much of anything., as if it needed more. Both Grace and Ish were back in the same area, and although they had a bond which death could not separate but instead united them, they lived their lives as if they did not even know one and other. It was the preferred, and safest way for both to exist.

Besides, the new century was upon them, and both had hoped change was in store. Life needed to deal them a strong hand they could play, but at the start of the new year, sadness would strike the Heald family once again without warning.

Chapter 13

* * *

In the surprisingly cold, bitter air of March 1900, a man who was loved by so many, a respected man who brought his family to the growing steel industry town of Conshohocken to give them a better life when the opportunity presented itself, took one final breath of air through his lungs, and quietly passed away in early morning hours.

It was a Wednesday with little significance for most, but for the Heald family, a patriarch had left his kin behind with lessons he taught over a lifetime, and rejoined the love of his life, Bridgett.

Old Ish had never felt himself after the vicious attack put on him by the much younger and stronger man Amos, and although he was a tough man by nature, his old age did not allow his bones to heal as he needed them to. It was the belief of many that this was the result Amos had been hoping for, only a few years later than he had tried. Once again, William would need to cope with loss, but more importantly, find a way to tell his younger brother that while this happened, and while he may seek revenge for the death of his father, he had to remember that their dad had not wanted this life for the younger Ish, and would be proud if he could keep his composure and see through this without ending up in jail.

But telling Ish what should be done and having Ish follow those directions were two entirely different things. Besides, now that Ishmael was back on the devil's drink, it could prove to be quite an impossible task. He was a damaged soul that seemed to have given up hope of finding good over bad.

Grace had heard the news from her son, William, and went quickly to tell Amos. Old Amos grinned, and responded to her with a look to the heavens, crying out,

"I told you, you old son-of-a-bitch I'd finish you."

He had.

But now Amos had to be cautious once more and watch his every step. Not only did Big Ish lose a daughter less than a year ago, but now his father was dead, and emotions were sure to be high for the big fella. The man had his limits as any man would, even if he was trying desperately to stay out of jail. And Amos knew that steel workers on the drink were not the type of men to play around with, and had killed over much less.

He tried to stand proud and firm in front of Grace, acting as if nothing was going to scare his soul, but deep inside, even Grace knew the carnage her ex-husband could cause if and when the time came.

She told her son she was sorry for their loss, and to tell his father she sends her best wishes, even if he doesn't want to hear it or doesn't believe it anyhow. William assured her he would pass it along and promised to try and keep his father calm and sensible. William was not the fighting type, and sometimes wondered how that trait had passed him by, but he was glad it had. He could not understand how a man could get such pleasure out of beating someone until you both bleed.

Back in Conshohocken, the family was preparing for their final goodbyes, and agreed to bury Old Ishmael in Gulf Christian Cemetery, which was just on the outside of Conshohocken in neighboring West Conshohocken, also known to the locals as West Conshy.

The interment was simple, and few attended. Big Ish stood there looking out over the rolling hills of the town below, remembering a time back when he was a young boy, and his father's lessons that he carried along for a life with him from those early days. He remembered stories of how his father lost his foot from the ankle down and had to find a new path in life. How he prayed over moving his family north with no idea of what lay ahead, and how proud he was purchasing his first home here through his hard work. He could see his father back in 1869, both proud and excited for opportunity and ready to give his very best to the mill that employed him. It was what his father did best. He gave.

Now it was his turn to decide what was best for him

and his family, but that is where he suffered most. His wife was gone, and his only daughter, murdered by the hands of someone that he possibly knew, and certainly not by her own hands as he was told. His body was wearing down, and not as whole as it was back in those younger years. Life had taken both a chunk of flesh and spirit from this man, and he was tired and sometimes, just ready to quit.

But he remembered his father's words, and it taught him that he could do more, if he would just let go of the past. His father told him once,

"You will leave many things behind for a reason, Ish. Even if you have no idea why. You don't need to retrieve those items. You need to know it's okay to lose, but it is not okay to live on that loss. Loss of something simply means gain of something else."

For Old Ish, it was the loss of a foot and the ability to work the farms that allowed him to move his family to a new place and a better chance at life. He was proud of the strong boy his Ish turned into. He was certainly proud of how William was creating a legacy in law enforcement, and the family man he had become while doing so. He loved all his grandchildren dearly, and when Mary Agnes passed on, so did a piece of him.

So in their eyes, they all saw him back with his wife, and his beautiful grandchild who had left this place suddenly. It was the way it was meant to be for those who carried such strong faith and to question it would be an act of defiance of God.

William was on patrol one evening, when he was suddenly alerted to a disturbance some blocks away, and he quickly enlisted one of the other patrolmen on duty that evening to go with him to see what was going on. They hurried themselves, following the young man who had stuttered words barely distinguishable, but still enough to spell out that terrible trouble was ahead.

When William arrived, the streets were filled with screams in pain and awe. Men were shouting obscenities with chaos behind their words. There were rows of big, strong steel workers from all different neighborhoods, throwing their hands in the air as if they were cheering on their favorite prize fighter of the time. But it was not a prize fighter. It was not someone who was paid to entertain the masses for the simple pleasure of passing the time by hitting a man on the head and body until he dropped. It was Ish.

For some uncertain reason, Amos had wandered a little too close to where Ish was back settling his father's affairs, and after a long night of heavily drinking whiskey, Big Ish had spotted him through the opening of a saloon door.

Without a single hesitation, and without a word to those men whom he was drinking with, he darted outside, rather quickly for a man with one good leg, and latched himself onto Amos as tightly as could be, ensuring that he would not get far this time.

He had blood on his mind, the look of an insane man in his eyes, and his hands were looking to drain the life from Amos. He blamed him for the death of his elderly father, and for fabricating a story about a man that, in Ish's mind, did not exist in Philadelphia, but threw off the police from finding out what had really transpired to his one and only daughter on that dirt and brick street in town.

Before Amos could gather his senses about what was happening to him, Ish was attacking him with big left and right hands, as if a mad-man had possessed his soul. The men of Conshohocken were cheering him on, no matter what mill he might be working for at the time, or what neighborhood he was a part of. For this moment, they were just men sharing in a common goal; all watching a little bit of street justice being handed out, as needed.

By the time William and the other patrolman had arrived, Amos was out cold, laying on the dirt below, probably having not a clue of what had happened. Ish was standing over him, his hands covered in the blood of two men and his eyes full of a demon, waiting for Amos to wake so that he could deliver another brutal beating and knock him unconscious again. But he was not gaining consciousness anytime soon.

William came shouting to break it up, and pushing his way through the crowd of rough, mostly drunk men, he should have been worried for his own safety for wanting to ruin the onlooker's entertainment prematurely. But he was not. He was worried his brother would kill that man and end up in jail for murder this time. Surely, if Ish had wished to kill him, he could, and there was no doubt that he would in William's mind.

"Ish! Ish! That's enough. Listen to me," William screamed as he gained ground.

The other officer grabbed onto Ish out of duty and without hesitation, and was thrown into the air and onto his head, just about knocking that poor man out as well.

"By God, Ish, knock that off! Listen to me, brother. Please, listen to me," he screamed at him.

Ishmael looked at his brother, and back down to Amos in his own blood below. He bent over, grabbed at his limp body, picked Amos up over his shoulder, and carried him to where a horse trough was nearby. Ish held him over top, and dropped him below, right into the water, and stared at him without saying another word.

William placed his arm onto his brother's shoulder, and begged of him to stop.

"Ish, enough. Enough. You handled your business. Now, come with me, Ish. Come home."

He finally did what his brother had asked, leaving the other patrolman, who had cleared his head once again, to clean up the mess.

As William and Big Ish walked back, the crowd of onlookers cleared a path for the two brothers. They respected both men for very different reasons. William, for being fair and just, and Ish, for handing out justice when it was most deserved. Most times the men of the town did not believe true justice ever won, but tonight they felt it had finally done so.

The crowd slowly left that night, aware that as men, they

fought for many reasons and over the simplest of things. But they had witnessed something that was long overdue, and saw a man serve extraordinary karma onto another man so deserving, without so much as an ounce of fear, regret, or penance. Ish did not care what the carnage he left caused him later in life or in the next, because in his mind, that man walked the earth when he ought not to, and if he took his life, so be it. So be it. Not all men deserved a chance to roam God's wonderful creation.

Chapter 14

* * *

Amos would somehow survive, and although his initial reaction was to march down to the police station and press charges with the local authorities, he knew better than to do such a foolish thing. This was a fight amongst men, and it would not look favorably on him if he tried to have Ish jailed for a beating a grown man most felt was well-deserving of that beating. Men would surely look down on him as a yellow coward, and he would possibly face more battles for doing such an unmanly thing.

Not to mention Ish's brother, William, was well liked and respected in both the community and the police force at which he was employed. If it was his word against that of the brothers, including one that wore a badge of law, he would not fare well. Witnesses would not come forward in defense of Amos, and he knew that for certain.

As he recovered, slowly nursing his wounds over the next few weeks, he took his anger out on Grace, accusing her of stealing his money, not doing enough around the house as he claimed she once had, and for anything else he could make up in his frustrated mind to justify his soaring temper. He was bitter and wanted revenge, but unlike what he had done to Old Ish, he was not going to overtake Big Ish easily. Even while heavily on the drink, he had enough sense to know he did not stand much of a chance.

So he would just need to move on from this, and figure out what was next for him in life. There are things just not worth fighting for anymore, and for him, this was one of those times he just had to move on, even if it was damn hard to.

Grace was very unhappy with how life was going with Amos, but she felt as if she had very few options. She was worn down from the daily grind and the loss of her child, had started heavily drinking herself, and had little to her name to offer anyone to court her. Her life had gone from hopeful as a small, curious child exploring this new country with a sparkle in her eyes, to dismal after what she had seen while here, and how she had lived to this point.

She would go back and forth between her sister's home for a week or so, and then she would visit with her brother, Dennis, who was the well-known track-walker.

Dennis was himself a larger man, built for the grind of the tougher life, and had been friendly with Big Ish for several years. He tried not to interfere with the divorce and the hatred Grace had, as he felt overall that Ish was an all right man outside of marriage.

As for Ish, he had put as much of the past as he could

behind him, aware that had his brother not been there that night, or had this occurred in any other town, the results would have been very different. He would be in jail most certainly awaiting a trial, because he knew that without the voice of reason from his brother, he may have not been able to stop himself, and Lord knows the blood-thirsty men that were there to witness his revenge, would have preferred to see Amos finished off, even if simply for pure entertainment.

William was worried that in helping his brother, it would cause him trouble at some point, but so far, no one batted an eye. He was back to his regular routine, walking the streets of town again, waving proudly to those who would wave back, and keeping an extra eye on those who preferred not to be seen by anyone.

On occasion, the two brothers would take a train into the city, and head over to the place where Mary Agnes had been buried beneath the earth. It was hard for Ish to accept that she was gone, even after a year had passed him by.

"William," he began, holding himself from letting a well warranted cry out,

"I should have been here for her as a father does, and I wasn't. She needed me most, and I knew her decisions were not the best, yet I did nothing to stop them, because my decisions were also not the best," Ish said.

William knew he was right, even though he was in pain and suffering deeply. He should have been back home more, and watching out for her as a father should do for his child, but no one, not even with the dangers of working in a place as she did, saw this coming. And to be fair, they did not know why she was singled out, and by whom she was singled out. Had they a proper suspect behind iron bars, well, things would be very different. A motive would be most likely presented, and eventually, folks, like Ish, would be able to come to terms with the loss, no matter how senseless of an act it was. For he would have some sense of closure, even if he carried the weight of the loss for his remaining life.

But short of an explanation that would mean little anyhow, doubt would forever cloud the mind of a broken man. He would suffer for the years he had left, wondering, "what if?"

His son, William, continued to keep to himself, and would not address the loss of his dear sister. It was not that he did not care, for he certainly did. But he preferred to remember her for the happy, unique person she was when alive. He could see her smiling at him in the dreams he had at night, and for him, he would much rather imagine that she never left this place. He did not want to hurt for her life being taken as it had in such a horrible way.

The years had caused young William's and Grace's relationship to struggle as son and mother, to the point they were barely talking at all. William did not like Amos one bit for the man he was, and to see his mother with such a guy as he, was hard to witness for a son. Amos knew it and did not care none. He was more selfishly focused on his own life, and what it was he wanted from it, to care anything about a boy wanting better for his mother.

By the end of 1900, not much had changed in the way of the world as the country had wished. People struggled just the same as they had the year before. Men were still getting drunk and fighting at the same, normal rate, and women were looking for love so that they could have families of their own at very early ages. The biggest changes that the Healds could see was that family was important, but fragile as all hell. You could talk with someone one day about nothing in particular and read about their untimely death in the papers the next, with an obituary that was quickly printed to meet the deadlines of the next morning, and most often, full of erroneous information that would never be corrected, just as some lives were destroyed and never righted.

But still, there was a new century to enjoy in some manner, and folks looked forward to what it would bring for them, even if they were as dirt poor as they had been twelve months ago. They felt that change was inevitable, for good or bad.

New homes were being built, and new families were coming into the bustling town, providing a surprisingly welcome change in the neighborhoods that once ruled on their terms alone.

Ish had briefly spent some time back in Delaware after meeting another woman, but that was once again, short lived. He could not seem to find love for many reasons. His drinking was out of control, his temper when he was tested by any man or woman was once again ferocious, and he was not a man who knew how to keep a dime in his pocket.

But he still had his son, who was starting to himself, find the ladies interesting, and was pondering life one day as a faithful husband and a good father. He had not witnessed many marriages last in his surroundings, but he was determined to break that spell if it killed him.

By the start of 1901, Grace and Amos seemed to settle things down enough that she was staying with him more than she wasn't. Maybe he was, as he aged, starting to tire some of all the nonsense and the whiskey that accompanied it. Maybe he was going to be able to put the past behind him and clear a path for them to simply live in peace, which is truly all Grace ever cared for.

Maybe. Or maybe he was just pausing a moment for what was to come next.

Chapter 15

Throughout the early part of the 1900's, Amos kept mostly to himself, which was probably more out of embarrassment than anything. That man had never in his life been manhandled so easily, and it both confused him to no end, and made him feel as if he needed to prove something to those who witnessed the event that took place that late evening in Conshohocken. If he did not, he would never live it down.

Ish was back home for the time being, heading from one home to another, boarding wherever there was an extra room for him to lay his weary head after long workdays and equally long drinking nights. His brother had offered him some assistance, but Ish was a proud man, and preferred to live as he did. Besides, he'd slept in far worse places over his lifetime. The sort of places most people would beg to leave before falling asleep peacefully, he found the best rest in. But it did also mean that he had seen things most men would never need to witness, thankfully.

William was chasing brazen, and more often mostly stupid criminals while logging long, tedious hours as a patrolman. He was desperately trying to get ahead and build a name himself and his family, as he always had his sights set on grander things, whatever they may be.

One evening, William was summoned to a borough home on the avenues, where a woman had fired a single shot from her second floor window at some fool she claimed was stealing her chickens. When William arrived in full uniform, the woman fired a second shot that popped just past his ear, prompting him to duck for cover and give a yell for her to lay down her weapon immediately. She did as she was told, realizing that the man walking towards her home, now lying flat as a sheet a paper on the ground, was there to assist her, and not rob her any further of her precious poultry.

Instead of arresting the woman for nearly ending his life and making his wife a widow, William sat with the embarrassed woman and explained to her that while he understood her frustrations with the thieves, she could not go around firing terrible shots off at anyone walking towards her home, trying to separate their souls from their bodies, without good reason first. She understood, but still was red hot, exclaiming,

"I almost got 'em William. If I was just a slight better shooter, he'd be a dead chicken stealing thief, and you'd be picking bits of him up off this street."

William was just happy she was not a crack shot, or,

as he told her, they would be picking pieces of him up off the street as well.

Thankfully, William was also a very patient man by nature. Having five daughters, as well as raising a nephew as his own son, required a lot of patience. Even more so than being a policeman patrolling the town did, so, in his mind, this was the easy stuff to handle and came with the job he so loved. It was when he arrived home after those long days and interesting nights, that he felt the true testing happened.

Now that Ish was back in his town and finding work at the local plants doing whatever was needed of him, the brothers were able to spend more time with each other, as they had always envisioned they would when they were young men. But it turned out that life took them on very different journeys down entirely different paths, and they were just lucky enough to still have each other to count on through the storms of life.

Ish didn't talk much about his Mary Agnes, or how their father had passed on recently, or even about how he beat that SOB, Amos, from ear to ear for the trouble he had caused his family, preferring to silently deal with those times alone in the darkness of the most restless of nights. William knew this, and although he knew Ish could tell, he did remind him from time to time that he was still proud of his brother.

Hearing that was confusing for Ish, as it was he who was proud of his brother William. After all, he had married the woman he loved and stayed faithful to her all these years, creating a family that Ish could only dream of. He had not let their nephew go to an orphanage, and instead added to the family one more time, and ensured that the young boy was looked on as a son, even if finances were tight. And even though he did not like or respect the law much at all, Ish had to respect William for his dedication to his work and for the reasons for which he did those things.

Both brothers had very different reputations around town, and people often joked about how night and day the two were from each other. Some would even joke that Ish was certainly born at midnight in a thunderous storm while William was born on a pleasant early afternoon sun. But outside of close friends, no one would dare tell them. Even as Ish aged, he was still as strong as an ox from the iron work he continued to do, and with him drinking heavily again, you never could tell when words would hit those ears of his like a knife and frustrate the large man enough for him to bite back uncontrollably.

Grace had also started to change as time went on, and although her family tried to get her to leave Amos on more than one occasion, she felt stuck and so decided it was better to just stay and accept it as her life. She had lost a lot of time with her son, lost her daughter completely, and was just afraid to be alone as she was beginning to age. Grace did not want to end up alone and truly felt that change would come from Amos if she could just show him she was worth the time.

But Amos was back to his ways. The drink was causing

him to lose his senses more often, and when that happened, his hands would go freely with intended rage. The sad part was that often, if no one else was around, Grace was on the receiving end of his frustrations, and because she was drinking as well, those nights and arguments they had could go long into the early mornings. The longer they went, the more the chance was that her bruises would multiply.

Amos, on rare occasion, would apologize for his actions and swear it was the last time he would ever intend harm to her, but even he could tell the truth was not what was flowing from his mouth.

He was an angry, bitter man who was frustrated with the hand life had dealt him, and upon realizing he was indeed mortal, he began feeling as if he had to start all over and show those around him that he was still to be respected and feared. Only, respect was never something people would give to Amos, even if he could place fear into their hearts.

During the summer, Amos was wandering home through a neighborhood known for a lack of civility, and decided to position himself on a corner, looking for a target or two. Within a few moments, he saw his chance with a large man, clearly inebriated. But Amos was only interested in proving he was still the one man to fear in town.

As he approached the unsuspecting man, he wanted to ensure those around him took notice. He screamed at the poor soul that he was aware of his affair with his wife, and was there to settle this score once and for all as men did.

The man had no idea of what Amos was screaming

about, and who his wife was, and just decided to continue on his way figuring he was just another drunk fool. That pissed off Amos something fierce, and he ran towards the man, jumped on his back as he was turned away, and knocked him roughly down to the ground. Once there, Amos began raining savage blows down, just as Ish had done to him. He did not stop until finally, a group of onlookers had seen enough and decided to pull the man off the poor soul.

They started to tell Amos he was "gonna kill this fella for sure," if he threw one more devasting blow.

Amos was growing tired, and the man was out cold from the first blow that landed as his head hit the hard ground below him. All the other needless shots were for not, and probably caused damage to the man for years to come.

Amos stood over the beaten and battered soul, breathing heavily while looking down to the ground, and stated,

"That'll teach you to mess with another guy's wife, won't it now?"

But Amos knew this man did not know his wife. He had never really suspected the man of any misdoings, but he felt that having a good reason, even if not true, would keep other men from interfering and dealing a beating to him in return. Neighborhoods were important to defend, but even those gangs of men knew when a man messed with another man's family, that these things needed to happen to ensure some sense of honor among immoral people.

The man spent several weeks in the hospital, never

knowing why Amos had attacked him in the first place. He was simply in the wrong place at the wrong time and had been beaten senseless so that another man could earn back the respect that he felt was taken from him.

Grace could see that Amos was not going to let this go, and because she was attached to Big Ish in the first place, it would only cause Amos to resent her more and more. Even when she tried to tell him that Ish was useless and just a distant, past memory of nothing of importance, she could not appease her husband. When young William was there to visit with his mother, Amos found himself with an excuse to leave the home. It was partially so that he didn't need to hear about Ish, and partially because he knew if he lost his temper and attacked William, there would be little hiding he could do to keep from another whooping at the hands of his father.

Chapter 16

"Where the hell have you been?" Amos demanded of Grace.

It was 1904, and still nothing seemed to ever change. Grace was in a constant fear of being verbally abused for anything and everything, as Amos was being, well, Amos.

That same year, William had met a woman named Annie Kelley from the Norristown area. Annie had lost her father, Lawrence, back in 1899, at an early age to consumption. That was the same year William had lost his only sister, Mary Agnes. Loss was expected, but still hard on a person.

For William, Annie was all he ever wanted in a woman. She was petite and pretty, but a strong woman in both mind and spirit, and that made her stand out from others in her neighborhood. She came from hard-working men and women, whose own family had immigrated from the dense fogs of Ireland during the great potato famine that virtually changed the landscape of an entire nation.

Grace liked Annie, and although she was still trying to rebuild a relationship with her son, she was happy to see him building a new one for himself, and with an Irish woman to boot. Grace could not ask for more in a partner for her William, as she knew the struggles the Irish had endured, and how strong and determined they were to make their own mark in the world, despite the terrible odds and horrible treatment they faced for simply being Irish.

Whenever William could get some free time, he would visit with his Annie, talking with her about all the plans he had in mind, and, if she would have him, the decent life he would surely give to her and their children.

Annie was excited at the thought of having her own family, as she had envisioned a large brood of children to raise and love. Her father had several siblings, as did most of the Irish Catholic families of the time. They just didn't have much to do outside of working, drinking, and attending church on Sunday mornings.

But in late May of that year, William was woken from a deep sleep by a neighbor who had heard that there was an argument on George St, just a short distance from where William was living. When William inquired as to what that had to do with him, he was told.

Amos had been drinking heavily all Monday evening at a friend's house, and had asked Grace to accompany him. Everything started off well enough, but Amos had polished off enough alcohol to kill a small man, and then went for more. Grace, aware of his anger and delusions when he drank, tried to convince him to slow down for the night, reminding Amos he had to be at work in just a few short hours.

But Amos and Alexander Burnett, were just having too much fun to be bothered with anything else. He scolded Grace and told her to sit tight and mind her business like a woman should. Men were discussing important issues, even though, none of importance were being discussed.

At about 3 am, Grace had seen enough and was threatening to leave with or without Amos. And that is when things took a turn for the worse.

William was only told that his mother was taken to Charity Hospital and was unconscious. The details were sparce, but she was not in good shape at all, and he was urged to head on over and be by her side.

He arrived to find his mother, Grace, lying on a hospital bed, unaware of the worlds' happenings around her. She was battered pretty good, bruised about her face and torso, and her face a swollen mess, looking nothing like the woman she was only a day prior. William took her fragile hand in his and talked with her. He told her he was there and that she would be alright. She just had to keep faith that God would mend her and allow her to finish her journey here.

As he said that, he had to wonder if she would even care to. She had been in failed relationship after failed relationship. She had been abused by the man she thought was her love after her first marriage failed. She had lost her son because of Amos, and even though he was by her side now, she may not realize that. What if she just decided enough was enough and she was done with this place?

William was nothing like his father. For he knew if Ish was in the picture, he would turn hell over on its side to get to that man. He would not allow man, demon, or God to stand in the way of what he would surely hand down to Amos as punishment. His hands would be the only judgement delivered, and with fierce intent.

But for young William, it just was not in his nature. He could absolutely want to stomp old Amos around, but he knew better. He knew he was not the fighting man his father was. He did not possess the size, strength, or the mind absent of common sense, as Ish would often say, to handle business the way he truly wish he could at this very moment.

Now, though, was not the time for revenge, either. It was a time to ensure his mother knew he loved her and was by her side, to see her through this taxing moment in her life, and to ensure her that soon things would get better. Somehow. Someway. They just had to.

When an officer arrived, he recognized young William as the nephew of police officer, Heald.

"Son, you doing okay? Listen here. Don't you worry, boy. We arrested those men involved and they will have their day in front of the judge. You just focus on your momma," he said.

William was focused, but he was still unsure of what had even happened.

"Pardon me, but how? How, I mean, what happened? What did she do, and who are those men?" William asked confused.

Apparently, when Grace was standing to leave, Alexander Burnett tried to convince her to stay, at first by asking, but then by telling. Both men were inebriated and thought they were in full control of everything and everyone around them.

Grace, who had also been drinking, cursed the men and told them she was tired and had had enough of this morning and was ready to head out and get home to her bed for rest she badly needed.

Amos pushed her to the floor, and when Grace, who had had enough of his man-handling, stood back up to confront her husband, she fell flat to her face onto the hard flooring below. Alexander had hit her over the head with an empty bottle he had consumed, and Grace was nearly knocked unconscious.

She was able to regain her senses somewhat, and in her delirious state, saw the front door to the home and decided to make a go for it. She then was knocked to the floor once again, this time, for good. Her own husband, Amos, had picked up a hatchet that was laying nearby, and hit his wife over the head with it. As she lay on the floor, both men kicked her about, until the point she was nearly dead.

As the men eventually realized what they had done, they decided it best to summon someone that could get her out of the home and to care before she died there. The only reason for this was that Amos did not want to go back to prison. He knew the last time he was sentenced was for a longer time than any, and this, if his wife died at his hands, would put him away for years, or something much worse.

By the time help arrived, Grace was lying in a pile of her own blood, unrecognizable to those who knew her, and unaware of what had just transpired. She was transported to Charity Hospital, where she was now resting.

The prognosis was not good. Both doctors that were attending to the patients that day, had told William to prepare for the worst. It did not seem as if Grace would make it through the night, and he should think about making arrangements for the soon to be departed, if she in fact succumbed to her wounds.

William had asked the officer to ensure both men would pay for their actions, so that justice could be served for such a vicious and uncalled for act.

"Son, that part is out of my hands. If it were up to me, I would serve it myself with ill intent. I'd probably have a few men stand beside me and beat on them like they did to your mother. This way, they felt exactly what she did. But I cannot. The law needs to handle this one, son."

William wondered if his father would have anything to say about this. Would he step in and handle Amos again for beating an innocent person? He wasn't sure. After all, he and Grace did not get along and did not like each other. Maybe expecting Big Ish to step up and handle this was not what was needed. Maybe this time, the law would work and keep Amos and this other fella behind bars, where they both belonged for years to come. Maybe. But doubtful.

For now though, William took the doctor's advice and started to write down all the things he would need to do if his mother did pass. He realized how unprepared he was for such an occasion, but how now, being the only man in her life capable of such a task, he was needed. So he did just as he was told.

And then, waited, and he prayed. And through it all, he stayed by her side.

Chapter 17

* * *

"Amos Alexander, on your feet," the judge demanded.

Amos stood there, sober as could be, afraid of what punishment was about to be handed down to him yet again. Young William was in the seats to the right rear of Amos, begging in his own mind that they would toss this man off a bridge headfirst, but he would settle for a cold, iron bar cell and the key to be tossed off that same bridge for good. Neither of those things happened, no matter how much he tried to will them to.

Because Grace had seemingly recovered, by her sheer determination and Irish strength, he was saved a charge and not tried for murder. Even though an old hatchet and glass whiskey bottle were used, they did not try him even for attempted murder. He was simply a drunk man who made a stupid decision under heavy influence, the courts quickly determined. That was it. He was ordered time served, and released, same as Alexander Barnett. They were both free to leave, and told it was time to clean up their lives, or the next time, things could go very differently. Amos had now heard this a few times.

Justice was anything but just, and Amos had once again gotten away with his stupid, selfish, bad decisions. Young William was baffled, as was his mother, Grace, but she knew this time, it was over for the two of them. She would leave Amos, because if she did not, her life would surely be over at his uncontrolled hands. She was not going to allow that man to have that satisfaction. If he came after her again, it would not be as a loving husband and wife in a simple, marital disagreement. It would be a possessive man going out of his way to cause harm, stemming from a raging jealousy. Grace had decided to leave Amos for good, finally.

Ish was staying clear of their business, as he knew some things were none of his concern, but in the back of his head, he still wondered if this man knew more about the death of his Mary Agnes, or worse, had something directly to do with it. He just seemed to find trouble with Ish's entire family and his temper was terrible. It haunted Big Ish, but he desperately tried to get those thoughts out of his mind, for he knew if any evidence was presented to state such, he would murder Amos with his bare hands if he had to, and life as he knew it would be over. It was not an easy step for him to take, but one that was necessary.

"If I knew for sure, the ends of the earth would not be far enough to hide that man, nor would the devil himself have a chance at having him before I did," Ish would say.

Besides, his son was doing well with his girlfriend, Annie, and Ish wondered if the two of them would end up married at some point, and start a family of their own that Ish could spend time with. Just as Ishmael had once envisioned doing for himself, but sadly, his family was broken and destroyed. He did have a good relationship with his son, William, though. That was certainly something to smile about, with so little else in his life.

Grace was living once again with her brother, Dennis, and her sister-in-law, until she could find a place on her own once again. She was in no rush, though, and her brother was always welcoming of his sister. He knew the trouble she had found in this country, and he hurt for her.

Dennis was still a very proud man and had made a name for himself in the railroad circles over the many years he had worked for them. He was strong, fit, and extremely understanding. So she could stay with them for as long as she needed to. That was his promise to her. Plus, Grace felt at ease with her brother. She knew that Amos would have a hell of a time getting by him, and if he somehow managed to, it would only be over her brother's dead body. He was not a pushover at all, and she knew Amos knew this.

William was pleased that his mother was safe and staying with his uncle and aunt. He had no fear of anything happening to her while Uncle Dennis was on guard. He could rest easy and focus on his life for a change, and his desire to one day marry Annie. He just knew she was the one for him.

At the end of the summer of 1904, Annie came to William with some news that would change both of their paths. She was carrying William's child, and expected to give birth sometime in April of the following year.

William, although happy, was not really ready for this all. He was still just a 21-year-old young man, trying to figure out what he wanted to do in life, so that he could support Annie and any children they would have together when the time was right. But now, he would need to take whatever job he could to ensure he took care of his responsibilities.

Both Ish and Grace were happy for the young couple, but nervous as well. They knew what happened to them when they had their own first child out of wedlock. The struggles, the arguments filled with anger, and the resentment that followed. They did not want William and Annie to make a quick decision based on her pregnancy and end up divorced, struggling and fighting as they both had for the short time they were married.

So Ish decided to sit down with his son, and have a heart-to-heart. One that he knew was long overdue, and perhaps needed now more than ever.

"Son, I know where your heart is, but I also want to ensure you know where your mind is. You need to keep some sense about you and listen to someone that has been there and knows the bruises that life hands you. Annie, she's swell for sure, but be sure she's the one for you," he started.

As he stared off into the distance, it was almost as if he was looking back on his own life, and the decisions he had made when he was once a young man, finding his own way through life.

"I've made my share of mistakes, and I've been to places no man should ever need to go, but I am still proud of the young man you are. So, I have at least that to look at in my journey."

William knew his father had struggled with many things throughout his life. He was a tramp for many years, never really finding a place to call home. His drinking had become sometimes so severe that his father would wake up in a cell, unaware of what had taken place the night before. There was the time he tried to steal a ride from Lancaster to Conshohocken, only to leave a part of him there forever. And then, the worst part of Ish's life, the day he lost his only daughter, for which he still had no closure.

His father would rarely talk about Mary Agnes, and it was for his own good. He loved his daughter, but he knew he was not there for her like he could have, and more importantly, should have been. This haunted his father, and William could see the pain in his face anytime her name was brought up.

When his Uncle William would come over for an occasional visit, and would mention some poor, young girl being left to die on the streets, a stranger that neither he nor Ish knew, it would bring back the horrors of that day he was first told of her death. It was haunting Ish and would for the remainder of his life, everyone figured.

Silently, though, Ish had sworn to himself that someday,

somehow, he would find out who killed his sweet child, and have his final revenge. He just needed to know for certain who was behind it so that he wasn't destroying his life for the wrong reason.

Ish was getting older, and although he was still feared for his incredible strength, the years of heavy drinking were taken a toll on his mind and body, and he was now unable to slow the process down, despite those that loved him asking him to save himself.

By the following year, on April 10th, 1905, William and Annie had their first child, and they named her Marion. She was the love of the young couple's lives, and although they were still unmarried, they knew this was the start of the rest of their lives together, and committing that to each other in a church in front of those that loved them, was simply a formality for the two love birds.

Ishmael and Grace, who had both survived tragic, near-death experiences, the loss of a beautiful child, and countless other rough patches through the sands of time, including surviving each other, had become grandparents for the very first time.

Perhaps things were changing for the two of them, even if only for a little while. They could only hope the worst was behind them.

At the same time, just a few short months after the birth of Marion, Amos was arrested for disorderly conduct once again, but this time he took things a step further. After spending two nights in jail, Amos was put before Burgess

Nuss for sentencing, which more than likely would have resulted in nothing more than time already served and a minimal fine. But in true Amos fashion, he could not keep his cool.

While the Burgess was about to start the hearing, Amos lashed towards him, smashing Nuss in the face with a hard blow, opening a gash that bled down to the court's floor. Two officers, quickly realizing what was happening, gave chase, springing towards Amos but missing him.

Amos had managed to flee the hearing room, and took off towards the river, where several squares away, he was finally recaptured and brought back once again.

But that was it. Amos went from time served to having to spend sixty days in prison, and was fined the sum of ten dollars. It just seemed he would never figure out how to live in a civilized manner, and no one seemed safe when he was at his worst. Even the ones in charge of the sentencing handed down.

Chapter 18

Marion was the center of life for the two new, young parents, and eventually, in October of 1906, they made it official. The ceremony was attended by only a few, and short in time, but was done with the traditional Irish Catholic mass, which was a must in Annie's eyes. She knew having a child out of wedlock went against all she was taught, but she figured at least she was attempting to make it right by making the marriage official in the eyes of the church.

Ishmael had celebrated his son's wedding by drinking the night away, and although he appeared happy for him, there were those that knew this man was struggling awfully. His brother had decided to pull him aside and check on his well-being.

"Fine day we had, Ish. Fine day indeed. Your son, well, he picked a heck of a gal, didn't he?" William asked.

Ish was once again quiet, probably preferring to be alone, but he knew William was just doing what brothers do when they are concerned.

"Yes, she's something. I'm proud of my boy. He deserves to be happy in life for certain," Ish replied.

He was clearly fighting with those demons once again, pushing back as best he could against his mind and his heart to keep them at bay, but failing as per his usual. William wasn't sure if it was the liquor, or the questionable decisions he had made throughout his life that were bringing Ishmael to a point where he could no longer escape his own destructive thinking.

"You all right, brother?" William asked.

Ishmael sat there for a moment, trying to pull himself together enough to show William that he was good as could be. He was a true man in every sense of the word; strong and determined, but even when he was suffering, he was able to hide that well enough that no one worried for him. If it was one thing that man could not stand, it was people worrying about him. He was able to handle anything that came his way come hell or high water, and this was no different. Only, even he had no idea what was pulling at him like a dead weighted anchor to the bottom of the water.

Eventually, he saw William and Annie sitting at a table, talking as if they were the only ones in the room. You could see the attraction they had for one and other, and clearly, you had to admit, they were built for each other. That was simply undeniable.

"William, look at my boy. He's proud. This is a grand

day for him, so let's just allow him to have that, all right?" Ish responded with a hearty pat to William on the back.

His brother, William, smiled, knowing fully well that Ish was deflecting so that the conversation would end, and while he was concerned for him, he also wanted to respect his privacy and his right to suffer alone in silence, if that was what he chose to do.

Grace was holding Marion somewhere off in the distance, singing an Irish song to her that her father sang when she would cry as a child, while staring into her tiny eyes to send her a message of love. She was herself suffering, but she was not going to let that impose on this day for her only son. She had not spoken a single word to Big Ish all night and did not plan to.

For years, both Grace and William had struggled with their relationship, mostly due to the doings of Amos, but even with him out of the picture, they had not had the opportunity to repair the damage that was done already. It would take some time to heal past wounds, but Grace was sure in time that would happen.

Now with young William having a family of his own, she hoped that the wrongdoings of her and Ish would teach the young couple how not to live. It had made little sense to fight for so few reasons to live as they had and to end up where they were, so now the lessons were not in what they did, but in what they had not done, and that truly mattered most.

Annie had asked William about his past, but she treaded

lightly. She had heard the story of Mary Agnes, as most folks in the neighboring towns had. It was big news when she died. Everyone, including Annie, had their ideas on what had taken place that fateful day. Most people conjured up far off stories of a gang of hooligans who had just been out for trouble and found it. Some blamed her lifestyle and felt she had gotten what she surely deserved for the sins she committed. Yet for a few, those that were close enough to the Heald family to know them somewhat, their thoughts on that day were more realistic.

Amos Alexander's reputation was not gained by accident. He was a troubled man, who seemed to attract drama like a magnet. No matter what was happening in the world, if there was trouble, and Amos was within shooting distance, there was a strong chance he was involved in said trouble.

The fact that no one could find evidence strong enough to support their claims did nothing to sway their minds. He had something to do with that poor girl's death, and only she and he knew it.

Amos knew there were plenty of people who believed he was responsible, and although he maintained his innocence, even he had to understand why he would be a suspect in the hearts of so many people. He was the last to see her as he walked her towards her home. He had been released from prison immediately prior, and had caused a massive issue within the family on his return. And no one, other than he, had seen any other suspicious, well-dressed, dapper man anywhere in the area.

It was something he knew he would carry the rest of his life, and it caused him to grow angry, and more resentful, and to drink so that he could care less about what others had decided for themselves. There wasn't an arrest made, and nor was there any questioning of him as a suspect by the police who did the investigating. Grace had not even questioned him, outside of what he had seen and what the man who walked her away from him looked like. The coroner made a ruling, and the police did their part in tracking down what they could. The end.

But as Grace got away from Amos, she began to wonder if she had been duped into believing the man out of love or possibly fear. Could she have defended a cold-blooded killer, who took the life of her only daughter? Mary Agnes was closer to Grace than anyone else, and because of that, Grace felt lost. Maybe, she thought, she had wanted, no she had needed love so desperately after her child moved on from this place, that she was willing to trust the only other person who said he loved her.

At her son's wedding, there were a few times where she almost convinced herself to pull Ish aside, and look into his eyes with her saddened ones, to ask if he thought Amos had done it. Was that part of the reason that Ish beat her partner so bad that he almost died from his injuries? Had he suspected it all along and just kept it to himself for purposes only he knew? And what if there was a way to truly find out. Could the police be talked into opening the case once again, so that possibly new theories could be presented, when she was not so blinded by hope?

But she decided against it. What difference would it make if he had thought so? The reality of it was that the case was closed, and the police didn't appear to have a care in the world about finding the killer. It was as if they truly believed and had convinced enough people that she had ingested that poison herself, because of some lovers' quarrel. And that was that.

Grace had learned to move on from Mary Agnes as she had little other choice, and she had learned to pull away for good from Amos, so there wasn't much left to do but to live out the rest of her life with her grandbabies, rebuilding a relationship with her son, and hopefully one day, finding someone to love her as much as she would love them back.

Chapter 19

* * *

Big Ish was off once again, but this time, he was heading west to a town in the middle of the state of Pennsylvania known as Mifflintown. Being offered a steady job was more important to him than where it was located, and he wasn't picky just as long as it paid steady and he had a place to lay his head. He was and would probably always be the definition of a tramp in his mind.

There was a steel plant known as *The Logan Iron and Steel Company*, and for Ishmael, this was an opportunity to start anew, and who knows? Maybe a change in scenery was what this tired man needed. It would certainly be a change in the usual crowd he was accustomed to being around, and perhaps that was a good thing. He knew that from time to time, you could grow roots if you stayed put too long, and Ish was not one for roots. He preferred the lifestyle of a traveler, where no one could pin him down for any length of time.

There were men from all parts of the state of Pennsylvania

who had signed on, and then men from neighboring Ohio were also offered positions a short while later, as they had orders that needed to be filled and quickly. This was going to be a melting pot of men and personalities, religions, if they had any, and different backgrounds. It would take a lot to keep these men in line, so the company also hired security personnel to help keep order.

But even with added eyes to watch over the men, Ish quickly discovered that this place was going to remind him of his hometown of Conshohocken, where he had spent many years creating a name for himself, or as others said of it, his legendary status of immortality. Maybe he knew a few of the men, but mostly, he was a nobody with some size. At first, he appreciated no one knowing of his past, and the life he had left behind became just a memory for him to hide away.

This did mean he might find himself in a position where he would need to show others he was not the man to play around with. Oh, he could be humble and reserved at times, but to push this man to his limits was like dancing with Satan himself, even if you were from a rough-cut past and born a steel man yourself.

Ish found out that just like he had done in Conshohocken all those years back, all he needed to do was to throw hands with a fella or two, ensure there were enough men around to see his incredible display of strength, and word would get around the camp quickly. And that is exactly what he did.

In late April, Ish was walking back to his shanty after

a long shift playing with steel, when he saw a group of about six or seven men standing in a corner area, taunting other men that were walking by. Some of the men would just continue on their way, and a few would occasionally swear back at the men, and then quickly realize the odds were stacked against them, and smartly carry on their way.

But Ish was feeling a little frustrated about the men, who were getting a bit louder, and starting to push the limits set by men in an unspoken set of rules. He knew he was not going to walk away from them as he had to go in that direction to get back to camp. So Ish thought to himself, if they see my size and still decide to take a chance, a chance is what I shall give them.

He keeps his head slightly down, trying to not be noticed, but also enabling the men to have a chance to let him by without any interaction at all. He could at least give them that. But alcohol must have been in the group's veins for some time, because not only did he quickly get singled out, but one of the group decided to knock the hat from on top of his head, down to the muddy earth below. Ish just gave a slight smile, but it was not a smile that one would give when a good solid joke was told. No. It was a smile that said, "You have no idea of what you have just done, and the hell you just awakened."

When he bent down to retrieve his hat from the drenched soil, the brave, or drunk maybe, man went in with his right leg in an attempt to kick the hat further from his outstretched hands, and as the other men were encouraging what was going on, Ish sent his message, loud and clear.

His left hand came up with such force, that when it connected to the man's jaw, a disturbing pop could be heard by all who were within ear-shot. The man had no time to understand the grave mistake he had made, and quickly hit the ground with a thud. His eyes rolled into the back of his head, and he lay twitching for all the onlookers to see in utter shock.

He quickly gazed over at the group of men who had just moments ago cheered on their brave fellow, and again, with a smile, headed towards them with no fear in his eyes. Two men tried to cut him off before he could get another powerful hand on them, but they were fiercely overwhelmed by the sheer strength of a bull that should have been left alone to feed in the field. Each fell like their friend moments ago, and each had only a split second to realize how stupid it was for them to have made this fatal mistake against this man they knew nothing about.

Once the remaining men had seen enough, they quickly left the area, and refused to turn around until they had cleared the eyesight of this crazy, smiling human. They did not want to chance him coming after them later if he could identify them easily.

Big Ish may not have been known by anyone up until this point, but word quickly was spreading about the man with a wooden leg who was stronger than the steel they were there to shape. The stories told by the other men of the camp ranged from the group of six being manhandled by one, to a group of twenty trying to fight off a lone stranger, who seemed to be not of this world, with the strength of ten bucking horses pinned in a cage.

Ishmael did not address the rumors, because he had no need to. He allowed the stories to get to where they would, knowing it had cleared a path for him to work in peace and more likely than not, allowed him to no longer need to worry about anyone testing him out. It was as if he had, with just a few blows from his hands, become untouchable. And that is exactly the message he was after.

One slightly younger man who had noticed what had happened, went by the name Henry Ennist.

Henry had run into those drunken fools on a few occasions but was much too fearful of what would happen if he stood up for himself. After all, what idiot would take on a group of six tough, drunk steel workers by himself? Well, now he had his answer.

He was camped temporarily not far from where Ish was, but he was hesitant to approach the big guy, not knowing what his temperament was like, or if he even cared to have any friends at all during his time here. But he did find Ish fascinating in many ways.

He worked at the same location, doing basically the same job as Ish, but he clearly knew that this man from Conshohocken had years of experience over him, and that he knew how to get around steel in the most powerful, yet graceful of ways.

Eventually, Henry decided to offer the big fella a drink,

and introduce himself.

Immediately, to the shock of Henry and many others, the two of them hit it off well. Ish was, after all, a decent human when those around him were good in return. He knew that Henry was a good man, and Ishmael figured what harm could honestly come from taking the younger man under his wing. Besides, it gave the aging Ish something to do, other than drink his nights away.

Henry would listen to Ish talk about tales of growing up in Conshohocken, and the trouble that often found him. His brother William, who was doing so well in the police force, was often a topic of conversation between the two, and Henry could tell the pure pride Ish had for that man, despite the differences they had in the understanding and respect of the law. He also could tell that Ish missed his brother when he was far from home.

Henry in turn would tell Ish about life out in Yeager-town, which was just a short distance from where the men slept each night. He, like Big Ish, was a drinking man, and that truly sealed the bond between the two men.

Ishmael received a letter just a few days after the fight he had stumbled upon, that his son, William, and daughter-in-law, Annie had a second child. Ish was the proud grandfather of another little girl that the couple decided to name Catherine. It always gave the big fella a smile, thinking about those two little girls his son was raising.

"It's the grandest thing, I tell you Henry. Even more grand than having your own children. Grandkids are, well, they are just different. Full of life that you can actually see from a short distance away, and not feel the burden you sometimes do as a parent. It's marvelous, really," Ish said.

Henry was a recently married man, and although he had turned 34 in the beginning of the year and had no children as of yet, he still hoped one day to have his own, and then who knows? Maybe he, too, would experience the feeling his friend Ish was feeling, about the grandkids.

The two men drank a toast to young William and his little Catherine, and Ish wrote back, promising to visit just as soon as he could get some time away from the plant. And who knew when that would be, exactly?

Chapter 20

* * *

As the months went by, Ishmael and Henry had made a few friends throughout the camp with some other tramps from in and around the state. Ish was feeling at home once again and was enjoying the feeling of the comradery that came with friends you could mostly trust.

The daily grind of steel work was backbreakingly hard, and led to drinking in the evening once the shifts were completed. It was a form of self-medication that everyone seemed to understand as a near necessity. Even though Big Ish had sworn to curb his drinking as best he could, he found himself right back in the thick of it all. He would consume anything that contained alcohol, even if he had never touched it in the past. He just enjoyed the feeling of not hurting more than the reality of being sober.

Henry had talked one evening about young William, and asked Ish why he never had any other children. That brought a sad look of almost defeat to the big man's face, and Henry could tell he opened a wound he should probably not have by simply being inquisitive.

"Ish, I didn't mean anything by it none. Just conversation, really. I'm sorry. I won't bother asking about that again, okay?" Henry replied.

But Ish wasn't angry with his friend. In fact, he felt a strange desire to open that wound up just enough if only to reminisce over his Mary Agnes for a few moments. He did not need to go into great details about her past and all that came with it. He could, however, tell of his only daughter, and how he had loved her but had not been there when she needed him most.

Henry sat stone quiet, listening to the man he called a good friend talk about the love of his only daughter, and how beautiful she was, and just how much she had to truly look forward to as she grew. But sadly, all of that went away one evening in Philadelphia, and there was no one to directly blame.

For a man who had learned to live with the fact he could no longer see her face in person, he was feeling like a wave of emotions was overtaking him. It had been almost eight years now since she fell on those streets, and her body let out its last dying breath. Eight long, lonely years filled with what-ifs and regrets. And here was Ish. A man who had fought his entire life over damn near anything and everything, had lost a good leg while breaking the law and stealing a train ride, and had been hit over the head with bottles, boards, and who knows what else, and he was still living and breathing as if those were all minor inconveniences. Yet, this beautiful child, whom he refused to see as an adult because she would always be his little girl, was buried beneath the dirt in the same city she had died in. It didn't seem fair at all.

But life was life, and the past was something we could only look back on with either marvel or regret. He had a new family to look forward to, and although he had lost so much in life, he also had gained more than he expected to when it carried on. His grandchildren would be his new focus on life. For years he felt that he had nothing more to look forward to until that daughter-in-law of his came along.

Ish appreciated Annie for many reasons, but mostly because of how she loved his William with a love he had never known. There was no doubt when the two of them entered a room together, the entire place could tell they were one. He had never felt that way about anyone, and although he and Grace had never truly connected on that level, he was starting to wish that somehow they had.

But he also remembered how his own father, Old Ish, spoke of the past and regret,

"You can spend your life chasing a ghost in what you feel you should have done, or spend it chasing the curious reality of what is to come. Nothing more, and nothing less," Old Ish had told him and his brother.

Ish had turned forty-five over the summer of 1907, and was starting to feel pains throughout his body from the years of wear he had sentenced it to. His muscles were tight in the early mornings, and by the end of the long, brutal workdays, he felt completely drained of a will to do much by the time the evening came around. To keep his mind off how he was feeling, he continued to self-medicate with the demons of whiskey, beer, and wine. That was his justification, anyhow. If you could pass out and sleep through the night with a little sense of relief from the burdens of the day, well, then why would one not?

Some of those nights, though, would go well into the early mornings of the next day, and somehow, someway, he would be able to rise at the first sign of daylight, and clean himself up enough to head back to the mill to be productive. There were those that marveled at how much alcohol he could consume in a single sitting, and still find a way to function throughout the entire next day as if he had not had a drop at all, and do it all over again.

It seemed to some that he was a legend among men, even if he had not intentionally set out to be one at all. He truly wanted to live a life worth looking back on, but somehow along the path he had shifted off course and found a beaten path that changed his direction for good, and he never found his way back on course after that.

"Henry, I need to head back home for a few. That grand-baby of mine needs to meet her paw-paw, and who am I to deny her of that?" Ish said to Henry.

Henry had become close enough to Big Ish by now that they were seen as almost an inseparable duo. Whenever one was drinking, the other was close by. If there was any trouble for Henry, the other men of the camp knew Ish was going to mix himself into the muddle at all costs. Even the new men that rotated in and out of the camp knew the story of how this man came into town and beat those stupid, poor obnoxious souls that were just out for a good time, or so the story was told.

To the men of the steel industry, fighting was just a pastime when there wasn't much else to do. It rarely had to do with wanting to hurt someone for little reason. Mostly it was considered "Just what men do".

"Can ya watch my stuff until I get back? Going to catch a ride later today and be back in a weeks' time, if that's all right," Ish asked.

The ride back home was scenic, through valleys and hills that Big Ish had seen many times over, but this time it felt different. He had a sense of pride as he headed back east to visit with his family. He even had purchased two small dolls at the company store to give to his grandbabies. It made the man smile and enjoy the ride that much more.

His son, William, was excited to see his old man back in town. It had been a while since the two men had time to sit and catch up about the very different lives they led. They wrote letters when they could, but rarely did those letters connect the men as much as being in person did.

Little Marion was growing her own personality and Ish wished to see that as much as he could. He knew from the letters that she was finding her way, but to witness that with his own set of eyes was something much different. It was pure and needed as much as a Catholic needed church.

This trip back home would end up being needed more than the big man would understand at the moment, for things were about to change course in not only his life, but the lives of those he cherished and held closest. It would be a final moment of ease for Ish in many ways, but for the time, he could only be concerned with what was directly in front of him that he knew was waiting on his arrival.

Chapter 21

* * *

The trip was short but sweet for Ish, and he cherished the few moments he had with his family as he truly wasn't sure when he would find the time to come home once again.

The upcoming workload was increasing and the men of the shanty community were growing frustrated with the conditions. It seemed at any moment there could be an uprising of some sort, but Ish figured it was men complaining about not much at all. He had worked hard and in worse conditions throughout his life, and this was nothing new.

But the men felt as if the longer hours required of them should come with more pay. They had a point, Ish knew, but they had signed on to do this work and if they didn't like it, they could simply get up and leave. He had always found some type of work that needed to be done, and so could the men there.

For a man who enjoyed throwing his hands at hard objects connected to a body of flesh, Ishmael didn't see

148

the sense in this particular battle. Perhaps it was that he was in a place in life where he felt things could potentially slow down enough, that he could actually enjoy the things he had always meant to, but never had.

Then the fall of 1907 came, and the conditions seemed to worsen still for the men. Many fled the shanties and went either back to where they were from, or found work elsewhere where the conditions were at least considered somewhat livable.

The men needed to be replaced, so a slew of new steel workers who were eager to prove their worth, came in from all parts of Ohio and further down south where the weather was unlike here. These men were not known to any of the current crop of workers, so naturally there would need to be a feeling out process, and trust would need to be gained by both sides.

Ish wasn't sure if this meant he would need to prove himself once again to these boozers from out of town, or if they were simply there for the work that was needed by the steel company. Either way, he figured, he would need to stand at the ready, just in case a throwdown was in the cards.

In early October, a letter came to the steel mill addressed to "Mr. Ishmael Heald".

It was written in such nice handwriting, that Ish could not believe it was for him, but as he began to read the words written so cleanly and purposefully, he quickly realized it was indeed meant for his eyes to read, and once again, Ish felt the joys of life being pulled from his body.

The letter was short and to the point, explaining that young Catherine, who was less than a year old still, had passed on suddenly. It did not mention the how or the why, but just said he should know she was no longer here, and Ish felt a chill come over his body, as if someone was blowing a cold breeze from across the room.

"Ish, what is it? You don't look so good," Henry inquired.

This man, who had found such joy in the eyes of his grandchildren, now was faced with the fact that he no longer would see her gentle smile, or hear her make those soft noises as she tried her best to speak to him as he held her in his massive arms. There was not a lot to say in response to his friend, and honestly, he wasn't certain how to say it any different than what it was.

"It's a letter from my daughter-in-law, Annie. Catherine is dead," Ish said matter-of-factly.

Henry felt horrible for his friend, but wasn't sure of what, or how to say anything. He wanted to let him know he was there for him, but how did this friend of his need him to be there? It's not as if he could do anything to help ease the shock or speak words that would make this situation any better for him while he wrestled with the reality that she was no longer with him. He felt helpless to his friend, who just twenty minutes ago was speaking of heading back for Christmas and what he was going to bring those grandbabies of his.

Ish didn't even have a chance to head back home to say his goodbyes, as by now the funeral had already happened and she was already covered under the soil back home, just as his own daughter had been. Once again, he felt a part of him gone and there was no one around to take revenge on. Not that it would make a difference, but at least he would have a reason to get things out of his system at someone else's expense.

For the next few weeks, all he did was work and drink. There were few moments of banter between him and his friends, and even less moments of anything that would resemble joy. He put his head down and worked. It was as if he was succumbing to the notion that no joy should be felt by a man with such a past as his, and to think that a future of happiness was to be expected was a waste of valuable time that he had spent too much on already. Life was as it was for him, and he could accept that or not, but it wasn't going to change no matter what his ultimate decision was.

Henry had gone back home more often, as his was just a short distance northwest from the camp. He preferred to stay in Shantyville, as the men started to call it, simply because of the friends he had made there, and the waking was easier when all you needed to do was walk a short distance to arrive at your job's destination.

By the time December came, Ishmael had not mentioned the holidays that were approaching, and Henry started to think this man was giving up on life.

"Ish, you planning a trip back to that town you from? You know, there are folks there I'm sure would be happy to set eyes on you, although I can't imagine why," Henry joked.

For the first moment in months, Ish managed to smile. He was tired, and defeated, but as he had learned, life went on as long as you had air in your lungs. It wasn't stopping for any man, so you had to live it out.

"I don't know about that. Perhaps a trip back would do me some good. Marion needs to see her paw-paw, and hell, these tired bones could use a little easing. Maybe I'll do just that," Ish responded.

Saturday, December 7th started off like all the other ones in the camp. The men were having their food, planning for trips back home for Christmas to see their families, and generally in good overall spirits. There were a few, though, that seemed to keep mostly to themselves and no one seemed to trust them much at all.

Recently, more and more men were complaining that they were the victims of theft, as they were noticing things missing from the shanties, and while that had always been a problem, it was more so now than it had been in the past.

This group of men did not speak as the others did. They seemed to have their own words and language, and although they worked alongside the other steel workers, there was something incredibly off about their mannerisms and how they spent their downtime alone in small groups.

Ish had a few run-ins with one of them in particular, but it always ended with the man moving on and deescalating the situation before Ish could figure out what his problem was.

Men began hiding what little they had in odd places,

including digging in the cold, hard earth below where they slept, just to keep their things safe from prying hands. Henry had offered to hold anything Ish needed him to at his family home, but Ish just wanted things close by. You never could tell when something may happen to a fella and then what? How would you ensure that you got your items back? Claiming anything was yours was easy. Proving it was an entirely different problem that he chose not to tangle with.

That day, Ish was having drinks with a few other men in the camp, including Samuel Nickels and Dennis McGuinley. Henry was tinkering with the idea of heading back home for the weekend, but was talked into hanging out with the men left behind for at least a little longer.

The men had kegs of beer, and were drinking all day, from sunup until sundown. They were teasing Henry because he was not partaking in the drinking that day, and they were hell-bent on having him join in. He just wasn't interested as he had been a little under the weather.

The beer was going down easily, and by the end of the evening, two kegs had been consumed by the three drinkers, and they slowly started to head back to their shanties to sleep it off. Just Ish, who slept in the shanty the men were drinking in, and his friend Henry were left behind.

"All right, Ish, it's getting late. I'ma head out. I promised my family I would stop by tomorrow. You get some sleep, okay big fella?" Henry said.

Ish was smiling, half asleep already from the long day.

He just waved Henry off, as if to say be gone. I'm going to catch some needed sleep and I'll talk with you later on when work starts for the week.

Henry left and Ishmael was dead asleep, when chaos came from out of nowhere.

The sound of the door opening abruptly early in the morning woke Ish up. He could not see for the darkness of the night had taken over the tiny room he called home, and the oil lamp was closed off for the evening as its fuel had been used up. The only thing he could make out with his extremely limited site was that someone was invading his shanty, and the last thing he remembered before falling fast asleep from the days drinking was everyone leaving so that he could get some much-needed rest. He knew he was alone once the last of the men left, until this moment now.

Ish grabbed the shotgun he kept close by just in case, and without saying so much as a word, aimed it in the direction of the figure breaking in, pulled the trigger, and then shot. A total of three shots were fired in the direction of the noise he had heard moments ago.

The sound was loud and obnoxious and woke many steel workers up from their slumber. It was not something one would sleep through, and for good reason. Ish was not sure if he hit the target, or just scared it off, as he was still half asleep himself, but he rose up, rubbing his eyes to get a better look and shouted for others to get in here.

A man lying on the ground in a pool of his own blood started screaming for help, and Ish knew he had definitely injured the would-be robber before he was able to take anything from him. He would surely regret entering that shanty. That much he knew for sure.

Samuel Nickels was the first man to enter after the shot, at just about two in the morning.

"Ish, what the hell was that? Are you all right?"

Ish looked towards the direction of Samuel while still clutching his weapon. Samuel had an oil lamp aimed into the room so that he could see, and realize the gravity of the situation.

"Dear God. This can't be," cried Ish.

Chapter 22

* * *

Grace was back home, spending more time with William and Annie, helping them through the loss of a child as best she knew how. She of course knew something about losing a child, and tried to offer direction while understanding the delicate nature of the situation. Not everyone handles great loss the same way.

For her, this brought back the memories of losing her only daughter, and how she wondered if she had never met that Amos, how would things be different today? She could not help that feeling of "what-if" no matter how hard she had tried to come to terms with the tremendous loss through the years.

Ishmael's brother, William, was continuing to log those long hours, adjusting to the ever-changing ways of his hometown. He missed his brother and those long, deep, into the evening hours talks they had when he came back, but he knew that he would return for the holidays, and so he had that to look forward to.

What he did not know was that Big Ish was returning much sooner than anticipated.

The train arrived in the early afternoon hours, and no one had any heads up that he was home. He walked down the street away from the station, talking to no one on his way to where his brother was living. As he got to the home, he took a long, deep breath in, and walked towards the door of the home William shared with his wife.

"Ishmael, what a surprise? We didn't expect you this early. Come. Come in, sit down," Mary said.

He walked into the home and said not a word at first. Over his shoulder he held a large sack, and had a box in his hand, that seemed hastily wrapped in paper.

"William is working as his usual, Ishmael, but I can send someone to fetch him and see if he can't come back to say hello if you like," Mary continued.

At first, he appeared to not hear a word she had said, but then he looked up, and nodded, realizing the question she had asked just a moment ago had not been answered properly.

"Mary, yes, please do so," he responded.

She could clearly tell her brother-in-law was troubled by something terribly, but she decided not to pry and allow her husband to handle it. She remembered how pained Ishmael was when his daughter had passed, and she knew of his granddaughter passing recently, but she could sense this was something entirely different from those two tragic events. It was a rare time when he would come into her home and not tease Mary about her husband in some manner. He was good natured with his family, even if outside of that, people could not see that side of the man. She knew deep down that he was a caring man who tried to do right, even when he was in the dead middle of doing wrong. He struggled for certain, and clearly was struggling now.

It took maybe an hour for someone to track William down, but as soon as he was found, he headed straight home to see what was going on with his brother. The day had been relatively quiet for Conshohocken, which was usually welcomed for him.

Ish was sipping slowly on a hot cup of coffee that Mary had just handed him, holding his bag close to his person, and not saying but a few words here and there. He was lost, and struggling to find anything to say other than the occasional, "how are things, Mary?"

Then he heard the sound of the front door opening, which at first startled Ish, and there in full uniform, as per his usual, was big brother William.

He took off his issued hat, aware by now that something was troubling Ish, and he set it down by the chair he sat in each night when his shift was finished. Mary, without hesitation, brought him a fresh cup of coffee, and told her husband that she was going to visit with a neighbor for a few, and leave the men be so that they could catch up.

William loved Mary. She always seemed to know exactly what was needed, and when, without hesitation. He felt as if she was the perfect complement to what he provided in their marriage and to their children. It made him smile, knowing she was forever by his side.

When the door closed behind her, William turned his attention back to where his brother was seated and looked at his face. He saw the strain of a lost man who was barely holding on, as if he were trying to come to terms with something so terrible, that William could only wonder what it was.

"Ish, what is it? What happened?" William inquired.

Ish did not say a word at first. He sat there in utter silence, but eventually, after a few seconds had passed that felt more like painstaking minutes, he took the bag he brought back with him from off his lap and laid it upon the table nearest to where he was seated. As he opened it, William did not take his eyes off Ish. He was studying his moves and mannerism, trying to gauge if his brother was okay.

Inside the bag, Ish took out the shotgun that he had molded into something that resembled more of a rifle. For all the years working with heavy steel and cold hard iron, Ish had learned quite a bit about the art of molding and constructing with the metals.

He placed it by his feet, and said to his brother,

"I didn't mean to. I honestly cannot remember much at all, and that's the God's honest truth. I...I mean, how did this happen?" Ish asked.

William leaned over and grabbed Ish by the shoulder.

"Whatever it may be, Ish, we will figure it out. Whatever it may be," William said.

He then pulled the shotgun off the table and placed

it closer to where he was. At least now that was out of Ish's hands, and he could focus on what news his younger brother was struggling to share.

"I was dead sleeping, to be fair, drunk as all hell and passed out, when I heard it." Ish began.

"The sound of something, someone, coming into my place where I was sleeping, and I don't know. I must've been startled awake from that sleep and instinctively grabbed it, pointed it in the direction of the noise, and fired. I can't say for sure, but that was what I was told when everything was over," he continued.

William was on his every word, using his ability as a law enforcement officer to read between the lines, and his love for his brother to grant forgiveness before knowing what for. One thing was for sure, this was not good, and he knew his brother Ish was in some deep trouble this time. He would need to learn more to see what, if anything, he could offer in assistance.

"What did you shoot, Ish? Who was it?" William begged.

Ish looked up at him and started to tear up.

"My good friend. I shot Henry. I swear to you it was an accident. I surely like the man. I would never, no how and no way in hell, shoot my friend. Not a chance, except, I apparently did," Ish cried out.

William sat back in his chair, going over in his head what he had just heard. His brother shot another man, and was back home, presumably running from the law from some other part of the state. This was not good, and he would need to hear much more before he could guide his brother in the best way possible, according to the law of course.

For now, though, Henry was apparently still alive, the last Ish had heard anyways when he first left. That was at least good news for him. Maybe it was just a superficial wound and everyone was blowing this into something it was not. Hopefully, no one was going to make much of a fuss over an innocent accident as they often happen, even by gunfire. That was all they could hope.

Ish sat there and talked with William until he had to get back to his shift.

"Ish, stay here for now. I will be back later this evening when my day ends, and we will, we will talk more. Don't you go anywhere for now, you hear me?"

Chapter 23

* * *

Back at the steel plant where Ish had been working before the unfortunate accident, there were rumors circulating around not just in the shanties, but also throughout the towns close by.

The story had changed several times, including the number of men present when the shooting took place. One man was telling those around that he was in the room and tried like hell to talk sense into the man who pulled the trigger, but to no avail. The problem with his story was that he had just arrived that very morning and could not have been near the scene of the accident.

Others were claiming that "a big fella," who seemed larger than life, had shot a man out of a fit of rage, and if it weren't for a dozen steel workers who finally grabbed ahold of him, well, more would have surely been killed by this crazed human.

But Ennist was still very much alive and talking. He was taken back home to Yeagertown by a wagon that Samuel had summoned at four in the early morning hours. Several surgeons were summoned and had tried desperately to remove the lead in his body but were having great difficulty. Despite the immense pain, they would try again when Ennist had some rest first.

Meanwhile, Sheriff Kemberling had accepted a man who declared he was turning himself in as a prime suspect, just off the trolley car near the middle of town. Ishmael Heald Junior said he could not recall the incident at all but was told he was going to be wanted shortly, and therefore he wanted to get it over with.

When he was questioned, he could not recall a lick of anything, and without Ennist pointing the finger, and no true reliable witnesses, other than the men who were creating these stories from thin air, he could not be held. So the good Sheriff decided to let him go, having no reason to hold the big fella, but told him,

"Be somewhere where one might find you, just in case."

Ish left immediately, and headed towards home in Conshohocken, but before he left, he did tell the sheriff of his plans to do so. He wanted to be close to family so that he had those he trusted close by. In this area, he knew men, but loyalty was a richness few could afford to find. It was not the place to be for a man in Ish's position.

The good news that came immediately preceding his departure for home, was that the doctors did not think the wound would be life-threatening, and that Ennist would make a full recovery in no time at all. This at least gave Ish some mercy, and a sense of relief that his friend would come through. The truth was, though, that Ish was so inebriated that he truly could not recall the events of that night. He was dumbfounded.

Back in Yeagertown, Henry was resting up with his wife and had his two brothers, who also lived with him, by his side. Both brothers had pushed several times for further accounts of what had transpired over at the steel plant, but Henry was just not going to talk about that. He was more focused on healing and spending time with his wife, while waiting for the doctors to clear him so that he could return to work.

But Henry would not return to work at all. On December thirteenth, in the same year of 1907 that Henry had been shot, he passed away at three in the morning. The large hole left in his hip was at first healing as hoped, but then uremia had set in just a day prior to his death. Ennist had been found to have Bright's Disease, which lead to the uremia, and ultimately, his final demise.

It was a shock to the family, the men of the camp, and even the doctors who had treated Henry and swore to his return to work at "any time now".

Ish had not been told as of yet, for he was still back home in Conshohocken, trying to figure out what to do with his life. Should he return to work and face potential arrest again, or perhaps give it time and allow for his friend to heal before attempting to go back. He did not want to cause his pal trouble, but he was concerned for him.

In the end, Henry spoke not one ill word of Ishmael, and nor did he ever point a finger at the man known as "Big Ish". He had remained loyal until his death in those early morning hours, and even if he knew more than he spoke about the incident, he would have never allowed for his friend, the one guy he trusted and admired more than anyone, to spend a day in jail over what he always felt was an accident.

But his family did not feel the same. The brothers, Frank and William, wanted someone to pay for the death of their brother. If he was not going to point a finger, they would press for the sheriff to do a full investigation and arrest any man they could, so that someone stood trial for what happened to their brother Henry.

William had been made aware of an arrest warrant while on duty, and had to somehow tell his brother that he would need to head back to Mifflin, turn himself in, and stand trial for what would now be murder. He was not sure he would be able to convince him to do as requested, and wondered for a moment if perhaps there was a way to hide his brother and save him from the trouble he was going to face.

But in the end, it would not matter. When he went back, Ish could tell by the look on his brother's face that something was not right.

"He died, didn't he?" Ish said as if he had already known.

"Give me a day to say my goodbyes, and I'll head out first thing in the morning, and surely turn myself in for whatever they said I did," Ish continued.

William, who was a strong, proud man, had water at the corner of his eyes, feeling as if he was about to lose his brother, maybe for good. The thought scared him, and pained him even more, for he knew Ish was a decent man, who allowed the devil's juice to control him when he could not. And he hated that addiction.

Ish went to see his son William and his wife, Annie, and their young Marion. He picked her up high in the air, smiled at her rosy, red cheeks, and told her,

"I will be gone for a bit my little chop, but don't you worry none. I shall be back just as sure as I leave here."

His son was worried for his father, but he knew that something like this was always possible with the lifestyle Ish was accustomed to. If beating Amos nearly to death had not taught him that getting away with things was only going to happen on rare occasions, well, this is where he needed to stand tall.

Standing tall was what Ish planned to do. He was a man of his word, and at about seven in the morning, he said his last goodbyes, and took a step onto the train that would take him back. As he did, he noticed his brother, William, in full uniform, had also stepped onto the same train.

Ish gave his brother with a confused look, and before he could ask what he was doing, William said,

"You think I would let you go back and turn yourself in without the support of your dear brother? You are a sad, mistaken man you are."

Ish smiled, gave his brother a hug, and thanked him.

He was scared for certain, but having someone there to ensure he was turned over properly, and without incident, was just what he needed but would never have asked for.

Within a weeks' time, a list of witnesses were subpoenaed, and jurors were chosen for the upcoming trial. They were hell-bent on moving this along as quickly as possible, while events were fresh in the minds of those that would be deposed. It also allowed for Ish to have a trial without having to sit by in the local jail longer than he would need to.

He was away from alcohol, and this allowed his mind to clear some so that he could replay that night over and over in his mind, to see if he could remember more. He tried like hell, even picturing the moment his friend had said his goodbye, right before he passed out for what he thought would be the entire night. He could not remember all the men that were drinking that evening, and nor could he remember firing the shot or shots that were apparently expelled from his rifle.

While he knew the evidence was lined up against him, he also knew that no one had actually witnessed the shooting, except for the one man who had died as a result, and that man stood loyal through his dying breath.

It made Ish miss him even more. He had rarely run into those that he could count on through thick and thin, life and death, and here he had, and that man was now gone at possibly the hands of the man staring back at him in the mirror.

Ish threw some lukewarm water on his face, rubbed it

into his deep skin, and through his thinning hair. He noticed he had aged in just the two weeks since the accident, and just wanted to get this all over with. He was ready to face the trial and witnesses, and either go back home for good, or head to serve out whatever sentence they may drop on him.

And so the trial would start, and his fate would rest in the hands of a judge and jury of peers, in just a weeks' time. On December 23rd, 1907, the Henry Ennist inquest, held in the grand jury room of the courthouse, continued all day until five in the afternoon, with a dozen witnesses present, and William seated amongst the other men and women who were eager to see the big man potentially responsible for the death of another.

Chapter 24

* * *

There were several issues at hand for the jury to look over, and nothing seemed to be cut and dry for the case against Ishmael Heald.

The question as to why Henry was wearing his overcoat and hat that was originally thought to be the reason he re-entered the shanty in the first place was not answered. He had apparently forgotten it, but by the time he was found lying in withering pain, he had the coat on his body. At first it was nothing to take note of, but the investigators who oversaw the case came across some interesting concerns.

For one, there was no residue from the shots fired on the coat, which should have been torn where the shot entered Henry's hip. For two, the blood that ran frantically from his body and onto the dirt floor, seemed to escape his coat altogether. Not a drop was to be found when they removed it from his person before trying to remove the lead that entered his body.

There was also the fact that no true witnesses to the

actual shooting could be produced. Either men were not talking about what they knew, or the ones that were talking could only testify to the fact that they had heard the shot and the screams for help but had in fact not witnessed it. One man swore he heard Henry say,

"Dear God, Ish. Don't let me die like this. Please."

Dr V. I. McKim was called to the stand to explain what he initially saw when he first arrived to help Henry. When he arrived, he said he saw Henry with a hole in his left hip that was about the size of the bottom of a teacup. He noted that a few steel men who were in the shanty attempted to help Henry prior to the doctor's arrival, but he testified that all but one had removed themselves, so he could not tell who exactly was in the shanty.

"The shots were of a good size and burned right through the very pants of Mr. Ennist. You could still smell the burned clothing in the air when I entered. It is my belief that a rifle of some sort, possibly a shotgun if I had to guess, was used to shoot Mr. Ennist at close range. Possibly with the muzzle of the weapon placed directly against the fabric of his pants that he wore that night," the doctor testified.

"Doctor, when you examined the wound closer, what did you notice?" asked the attorney for the prosecution's side.

"I saw that the penetration made by the projectile had gone in the hip muscle a considerable distance and rested in a knot as large as a hen's egg, near the pelvic cavity of the victim."

"And doctor, after you saw that, what, if anything, did

you do to treat the wound of Mr. Ennist?"

"I bandaged the wound as best I could under the conditions present, and prepared him for transport out of there," the doctor said.

The undertaker was then summoned to the stand and asked about his role in this unfortunate incident. The prosecution refused to call it an accident, as they wanted someone to pay for the death of this young man and knew their best chance was to call it anything but.

"I prepared the body for burial and found, while doing so, that the wound had started to heal. It was blood poisoning caused by the gunshots that had set in, and not the wound."

Ish could only sit there and listen as one by one, the witnesses recounted what they had seen, heard, or did that early morning of December 7, 1907. He was still unsure of all that had happened, but he knew that he was the last man to see Henry, and that they had recently decided to call it a night, or more appropriate, a morning. From that point on, he still could not recall a damn thing.

It was almost as if he was sitting at the very back of the courtroom, listening to a trial for some other poor soul and learning just as everyone else was as the questions were asked by the lawyers and the answers were giving by the witnesses. In fact, it could be just about anyone sitting there on trial, but at the end of the day, it was he, and he knew his life rested in the hands of the jury that was selected in such a hasty fashion, and all of which were from the same area as Henry. None of that seemed to give him a good chance at freedom.

William did his best to be there for Ishmael, but he knew his hands were tied. There was nothing legally he could do to help his brother out. The damage was done and he had to stand up and face the charges, which was exactly what he was doing. For that, William was proud of his brother. He had not run into hiding, and nor did he try to pass the blame onto another man in the camp to deflect blame from himself. He was called back, and he went back.

He truly believed his brother, Ishmael, when he said he could not remember a dang thing. There was no reason to believe his brother was lying about having no memory of any of the events that morning, and Ish was not a man known to fabricate a story. He was also one to stand firm and take whatever someone was willing to dish out, legally or not.

Sheriff Kemberling was brought to the stand and sworn in, before testifying.

"Sheriff, why is it you arrested this man, Ishmael Heald, and the reason he is here today standing accused of murder?" the prosecution asked.

The Sheriff sat straight up in the chair and cleared his throat. He was a strong lawman, believing that justice should always be handed out, even in the smallest situations and the pettiest of crimes. It was important to keep law and order, he always felt, and to hold someone accountable for their actions, no matter what the reason was.

"I had been told by a few men at the steel plant that

a rather large fella who went by the name Big Ish, had possibly been the one to shoot Henry Ennist. So I went to find him, and he must've had word by then, because instead of me finding him, he found me and surrendered," the sheriff started.

"Yes, and once he surrendered for the crime of shooting Mr. Ennist, what happened then? What did you do with him?"

"At first, I questioned him as to his whereabouts and learned that he was indeed in the shanty when the shot man had been found, laying in his own blood," the sheriff continued.

He bounced back and forth with the prosecution, and then one final question was asked.

"Sheriff, did you make contact with Mr. Ennist and if so, what was the result of that conversation?"

"Well, I did in fact make contact with one Mr. Henry Ennist at his home. I told him that I had arrested a man by the name of Ishmael Heald, and that he had turned himself in because some of the men had mentioned him as a suspect. When I did, Ennist would not speak more to me. That was it," the sheriff said.

"How did you leave it when you left?" the lawyer asked.

"Mr. Ennist said I ought to release the prisoner because he was certain I had the wrong man in jail," the sheriff finished.

One witness that was strong for the prosecution was a man by the name of George Beddow. He had been one of the first men in the shanty, and was the one who had heard Henry plea for his life.

George was asked about his position at the steel mill,

and what, if anything, he had seen.

"Well, first, I heard a man screaming as if he were dying. Woke me clear out of bed, it did. I ran over in the direction where I thought I heard the noise coming from, and entered carefully through the front opening."

"When you entered into the scene, whom or what did you see, if anyone or anything?" the lawyer asked curiously.

"As I said, I entered in as carefully as a mouse as I wasn't sure what I would find. I see Ish standing there, looking down at this Henry fellow, and no one else. Henry's clothes were on fire, and so I ran over and threw dirt onto them to put out the flames, using my hands to finish it off," George said.

When he was asked about Ish and his reputation, George seemed slightly nervous, but the prosecution pressed him harder to be truthful in all matters as to what he had witnessed.

"Ish isn't a guy to play around with, for certain. He is respected at camp, but also feared by many. He doesn't take nonsense from no man, and everyone knows it. He can drink more than most men, and on many occasions has proven that to be the honest to God's truth," George spit out.

"And do you know if Mr. Heald has or had at any point, a weapon in his shanty?"

"As a matter of fact, he did. He's one of the only men in camp to have a shotgun. He showed it to me once. It was fixed to work as a rifle but still has the blast of a shotgun. He did a fine job of making it," George finished.

When he was finished, Samuel Nickels was called as a

witness. He testified that he had entered the shanty just a bit after George had, and noticed that no one was trying to figure out what had taken place. Instead, everyone was attending to Henry, and Ish was standing nearby in a panic.

It was Samuel's belief that Ish could have mistaken Henry for a robber, and shot him without knowing what or who he was shooting at. He said he believed that the deceased was heading back for his overcoat and hat, because it was not on the man when he arrived to see what all the noise was.

"How did the overcoat and hat get on to Mr. Ennist then if it was not on him when he was found by you, shot, and screaming in pain?" the lawyer asked.

Samuel hesitated, looked over to where Ish was seated, and just let out with,

"I'm sorry. I have no idea. It was a crazy time trying to help him, and I did not take notice as to when or how that may have happened."

"Did Mr. Heald say who shot Henry Ennist?" the prosecution asked.

"No. He was terribly worried over the affair but could not provide any explanation. He was just worried for Henry. They were good friends, them two, and I don't think Ish would hurt him no matter how much they had to drink," he finished.

"Sir, state your name for the record," the judge stated.

"My name is Dennis McGuinley, your honor."

"Counsel, proceed."

"Thank you your honor. Mr. McGuinley, can you

please tell the courtroom what you remember of that early morning."

"Well, I had spent the night there drinking with Ish and another fella, can't remember his name at the moment, and Henry was there. We were all drinking, and tried to get Henry to join in, but he refused. So the three of us had two kegs of beer, and were pretty tired to the point I had to lie down to get my senses before walking home. I stayed a few, then got myself up, said a goodbye and was on my way."

"How was the mood in the room?" the attorney asked.

"The mood? We were all drunk, that much I can tell you. There was no fighting or arguing or anything like that, if that is what you are asking. We were just having a good ol' time, not causing any issues to anyone. There was no sign of trouble at all," he finished.

The final witness for the day was Henry's brother, Frank.

Frank testified that his brother had told him at home that it was Ish who had shot him by sheer mistake, and that he had no recollection of how it happened. He said his brother refused to give any further details, and that he swore to him that Ish did not mean for it to happen and to tell no one.

Ish was now sitting uncomfortably in his seat, aware that the evidence presented was little, but damning for sure. They had not a lot to go on concerning physical evidence, but several men had testified that he was in the shanty alone with Henry, was the last to see him before the shooting, and was the only man in the shanty with Henry after the shooting. He also had been one of only a few men with a shotgun in his possession.

It was not looking good, and still, the following week there would be even more witnesses to testify at his trial.

For now, though, he was removed and sent back to jail to await his next hearing, and William was heading back home to be with his family for the week and give them the updates they would certainly be awaiting.

Chapter 25

* * *

He'd been to jail more times than he could count, but this time? This one was different than the others. He knew that his freedom was on the line, and while he was struggling with the fact that he could face serious time, he was also fighting with the fact that Henry was no longer here, and he could have been the reason for his friend's untimely death.

He sat in the cold cell and tried clearing his mind of anything else but that early morning. He remembered teasing Henry because he had no desire to drink late into the morning while the other men did, but he knew Henry understood that it was all in jest. Never did he feel angry or frustrated with the man he called a friend.

Then he remembered the moment when he left in those early hours, and he knew it was time to get sleep because the next day was coming and coming fast. There would be planning to do for the coming week, and if there was a chance at any extra hours, he could surely use them this time of year.

All during the week he woke up in that cell, and eventually his body started to ache. The hurt from not having any liquor to settle his pain was starting to affect his joints and muscles. His mind was frustrated at him for not providing what it felt it needed to feel normal once again. Being forced not to have a drop of the poison that he had grown to love almost as much as life itself, was excruciating.

The police were growing to understand this man through their occasional conversations separated by iron bars, and they generally wondered if he did it, and if so, did he truly mean to or was it all just a horrible accident that happened when someone had too much to drink, and a fear of being robbed. They had seen this happen several times over the years.

Ish didn't appear to be a bad guy, but more of a sorry tramp that had found trouble more often than not. Life was rough for steel men and you had to be tougher than the next guy or things could go seriously wrong. They knew he had to put on a face when it was called for, but deep down, when he spoke of his beautiful daughter and her untimely death, and when he spoke of his son and grandchildren, the one that had survived and sadly the one that had not, he seemed just like any other family man.

One of the guards even thought about sneaking in some whiskey from his own stash for the poor fella, just to ease his terrible nerves a little with everything going on, but then he thought better of it. This would just make it start all over if Ish were to do real time in prison. So he would just need to suffer through and wait it out until his body and mind adjusted to the change.

The days went by slow, as Ish was used to working long hard days filled with loud noises and frantic workers, and enjoying even longer hard nights once that work was completed. Now it was just him, and those walls and bars around him, plus the occasional officer who was willing to talk. The ones that did not didn't seem to give a care about his condition, and Ish didn't blame them at all. While he didn't like or respect law enforcement outside of his brother, he knew well enough that this was Henry's town and that people knew his family.

By the time Saturday came, he was just happy to be getting out of the cell, even if he was trading that for the wood-lined walls of a courtroom that seemed determined to bury him beneath its floors. He was able to see some sun peering through the windows and a bit of fresh air for the time it took them to transport him to the courthouse, and for that little moment, he felt truly free.

But that quickly ended when he entered the room and saw the witnesses that were there to testify for, or against him. He looked around to see if William had come back but did not see him. He was alone today, and that was just as well. Who would want to travel all the way there weekly to see others talk about the terrible things that had happened? He was glad his son did not come, although if he had asked, he was sure young William would have made the trip.

There were many witnesses this day, including the

Coroner who finished his testimony, as well as Mrs. William Ennist, Henry's mother, and many other men and women, mostly steel workers and their spouses. But little evidence was secured as most of these witnesses were truly not witnesses at all, but people who seemed more interested in speaking theories rather than facts.

It felt like a waste of a day, but Ish again was just glad to be out of the jail.

One man's testimony, though, contradicted that of Nichol's testimony the previous week. He said that Ish was not worried at all over the condition of the man named Henry, and in fact he stayed around the other shanties prior to leaving for Harrisburg and then ultimately Conshohocken.

And once again, the trial was completed for the day, and the judge ordered anyone who was needed to be there the following Saturday to continue the inquisition. This was a matter not to be taken lightly, and with so many witnesses, the jury would need to be sure they heard from everyone, including the man accused of murder, Ishmael Heald. He had yet to speak, and would probably not until the final day, and the last witness was produced and finished with their questioning. But no one knew if he would testify on his own behalf, including his own attorney.

Ishmael was removed back to the jail and faced yet another week mostly alone. This particular week, there were more rowdy, drunken men in and out. Most spent a night sobering up, while a few others had a two-day sentence for fighting, or burglary, nothing like what Ish was in for.

He kept mostly to himself, but at times, a conversation struck up. Questions such as,

How'd you lose that leg of yours?"

Or

"You that big fella who shot that young man over there at shanty row?"

He tried to keep the conversation as short as could be, because he honestly did not wish to talk about the unfortunate crime he stood trial for week in and week out for the last several, and possibly the next several. Even though it was nice to have someone here and there to chat with, and it gave him a sense of being back in the shanties, it just wasn't the same.

One kid had been there for the better part of two days over a drunken fight he had while on the whiskey wagon. Ish could see this tough youngin as himself those years back, and he smiled when he talked with him.

"Listen here, son. It ain't worth it. All that fighting and drinking and fooling around? It catches up to you. It catches you for certain. My father told me to listen to his warnings all those years now gone by, and did I? Not for a second. Look where it got me, boy", Ish said, wishing he had listened.

But he could see there was no getting through to him, just as there was no telling Big Ish that harder days were coming if he didn't keep his head out of the troubles and out of the bottle. He just wasn't built for calm, but wanted to at least give the kid a few words that perhaps he would repeat to himself someday when he was at a cross road.

The week seemed to go by like those dark early mornings do, quickly as the sun rises without your permission before a man was ready to sober up for the day's work ahead.

On January 3rd of 1908, the newspaper told a tale in almost poetic harmony. It mentioned that that accused murderer, Ish Heald, was to finally testify for his actions, and that the entire area would learn if he indeed intended to kill the man in cold blood as some had suggested, or if it had been a mere accident after he consumed an inhumane amount of poison.

Henry was described in the paper as half frozen from the cold, and weak from the loss of such a large quantity of blood from a jagged wound to his hip.

They then talked about the weapon used in the sad and untimely death of young man, Henry. "A peculiar mechanism, modeled after the old style muzzle-loading Colt's Navy revolver of five chambers." Out of the five chambers, three were void of fine bird shot that Saturday, and found in Mr. Ennist' hip was that same fine shot.

Mentioned was his brother, Police Officer Heald, and the Chief of Police for Conshohocken, Chief Haines. William was the one who talked Ishmael into turning himself in, at least if you believed what the papers said, anyway.

Big Ish was described as being a man, large in stature, with a robust constitution about him. He had one leg removed below the knee, and walked with an artificial one to level him out. The writer of the article said there was not much more known about this interesting man, other than the fact he was a good judge of liquor. Even Ish would agree with that statement.

The trial continued and after a few more witnesses testified with little help to either side, Ish was ready to take the stand on his own behalf. His attorney, H. O. Lantz, did not want his client to testify, for fear it would incriminate him, but Ish wanted to get his story out.

Ish told of the terrible amount of liquor the men had consumed, and that each one in the shanty that late evening and early morning, had been having a grand ole time. There were no arguments amongst the men, and in fact, the same men had agreed to a night of drinking the following, if they had an ability to recover in time.

He was asked about what happened once he went to bed, and for the life of him, he said, he could not recall.

"I can honestly say, without any hesitation, that I do not recall seeing a man enter my place of slumber, and nor do I recall grabbing a weapon and firing upon a soul," he testified.

"I would sooner shoot my brother, than Henry. He was just like family," Ish finished.

When he was finished answering questions, the jury was sent out to examine what they had heard, and to come back with a verdict in the death of one Henry Ennist, whenever they had secured one.

They did as they were instructed, and within thirty short minutes, they had returned, exclaiming to the judge that they had come to a decision on the matter.

Ish was shocked at the speed at which a decision had been made, and wondered if the hastiness was a good sign or bad one. He had very little time to think about what was going to happen, though, as the judge seemed eager to get that decision out so he could officially close the case for good, either way.

Six jurors stood up from their seats, while one held a piece of paper in one hand and looked over to the judge for his decision.

"Sir, please read your decision for the court," the judge said.

"We, the jury, find that Henry Ennist was killed, but without any premediated intent. We find that the man responsible for such, is the man seated at the defense table who goes by the name of Ishmael Heald."

Chapter 26

As it turned out, the jury had a difficult time believing most of the witnesses that both sides had presented. They felt that the stories told by Ish's comrades had little to no merit, making hardly any sense about the suspected crime that had occured that cold December morning. Several of the witnesses appeared to be under the influence of alcohol while testifying, and the deception they shared about that night and into the morning hours seemed to run deep through their veins.

They believed that Ish may have grown irritable at the fact Henry was finished drinking for the night, and Ish wanted all of them to continue. He, no doubt, shot Henry out of a frenzy, both carelessly and without thought of what may come from such an action. Perhaps he only meant to make a scene and had not intended to kill or even hurt a soul, but ultimately that is exactly what he ended up doing by his reckless behavior.

Further, the jury felt that the testimony of the coroner

told a fascinating story. That the men in the camp rehearsed what they would say, so that no man would be charged with the incident. But the coroner was a smart man and had offered and bought drinks for the men after Ish fled the area. He was able to talk them into more accurate details and to catch them in blatant lies, the more they consumed. It was what actually put him onto the trail of Ish in the first place. It would not be admissible in a court room, their words under the influence of whiskey, but certainly it would bring forth a starting point for which he could place his accusations on.

Henry never felt Ish should stand trial, and that was the only doubt the jury of six had. How could it had been malicious if even the man who was shot and had died, did not want to single anyone out prior to his own death? That part stumped the jury, but only long enough for them to find their senses and their voice. Someone had to be held accountable, and Ish was the only logical person.

The only thing left to do was to decide on the sentencing for the accused. It needed to fit the crime that the jury had been convinced was committed, so another hearing would need to be held. For now, though, Ish was sent back to jail, and was finding himself awaiting the impending decision. He had no control over what would be handed down, and that did not sit well with him. He was a man who could fight his way out of just about anything, but not this time. His large fist that he was so good at using were not going to be able to save him, so he turned to prayer to a God who he felt had left him alone, as a last, desperate hope.

On January 18th, 1908, Ishmael was called back to the courts, and the judge ordered him to stand so that he may be properly sentenced.

Ish stood up, his head hanging lower than it had at any point, and then raised and laid his eyes upon the judge in charge. He was possibly hoping for some grace, but mostly expecting to be sent to prison for a considerable time. Afterall, this was not a fist fight where two drunk men were throwing down punches to prove who was the tougher son-of-a-bitch. This wasn't a situation where he could be justified in hurting a man with pure justification, and as it turned out, killing that same man.

The judge went over the charges presented before him and came to a determination.

"Ishmael Heald, for the crime of second-degree murder, upon one Henry Ennist, I sentence you to a fine of twenty-five dollars, and order you imprisoned in the Western State Penitentiary for the length of not less than two years and six months, ordered to start from this very day of January the eighteenth, in the year nineteen aught eight. So it shall be," the judge said as he slammed his gavel down onto the wooden bench, signaling the end of an emotional and sometimes out of control hearing.

His brothe,r William, and his son, young William, had both been present for the sentencing. They would not allow Ish to be alone while such a stressful and perilous day was at hand. Both smiled at Ish when he was led out, and told him that they would surely visit whenever they could get the opportunity.

It was a little comforting to know that at least his family still had love for him, despite the fact he was now a convicted murderer. In all his life, he had been known by many names and been called by many fitting and sometimes unfitting terms, but this, murderer, was something he would need to carry to his grave and into the next life, if God would allow for such a next life.

On the banks of the Ohio River, on just about 21 acres of land in the Pittsburgh, Pennsylvania area, stood a prison that was once used during the Civil War prior to moving to its current location. Known by some as "The Wall," it stood firmly in the cold air, Western State Penitentiary.

It was a massive, brutal looking prison that housed men from all over the country, and now it would be the home for Ishmael Heald for the next two and a half years. He was transported along with several other inmates, processed, and given a numbered uniform which he was required to wear. He was officially prisoner number 5928. When he emptied his pockets upon his initial entry, he had twenty-five cents, three small collar buttons, and one razor to his name. Ish was no longer a free-spirited tramp traveling from camp to camp and mill to mill. He had one home for the next few years, and he knew life was forever changed.

He was received officially on February 25th, 1908. His entrance paperwork stated he was Roman Catholic, although he only seemed to pray when he knew he was in a heap of trouble. It also stated his occupation was an iron worker.

His height was listed as six feet and one-half inches, weighing two hundred-eleven pounds. His hair was of a dark gray and his beard a sandy color with his eyes being slate in color. His build was marked as stout, and his tattoos labeled as the following: Bust of a sailor girl in blue ink on his left forearm, I H in blue ink on right forearm signifying his initials, and a small heart in blue ink between his thumb and first finger on his right hand, for his daughter Mary Agnes who had passed. His scars were numerous from the years of fighting, and of course they marked his right leg amputated six inches below his knee.

The first few weeks there, he was still feeling the effects of the detoxing his large body was undergoing from not having a drop of liquor. He had actually tried to bribe an officer who was transporting him, half-jokingly, for just "one more for the road". The officer just kept his same demeanor, pretending as if he did not hear a word from the prisoner.

Ish, who naturally made friends with men quickly, possibly because they feared him and preferred to have him on their side, was handling things differently here. He was alone and preferred to stick to himself. This, he felt, was justified because Henry had died, and he should not be able to enjoy any of the time he was spending here as Henry could not enjoy another day alive. His thoughts were of how Henry would not put any blame on him, even as he lay dying. That was proof that Henry was indeed the best, most trusted friend Ishmael had ever encountered in his entire life. And now he was gone.

As time went by, he grew lonely and started to write letters back home. His son, William, would try to write back, but more often was so busy working that he could scarcely find the time. Instead, Annie would write a letter a week on his behalf, letting him know how Marion was doing, and about how, eventually, they would try for another. She wanted some time to deal with Catherine's death first, which Ish understood more than most.

Ish was also shocked to learn that his former brother-in-law, Dennis Waters, decided to write to him. It was only a few times, but those times were powerful moments for Ish. Dennis wasn't really the writing type of guy, but he knew Ish was alone and he simply wanted to offer some encouragement to his old friend.

As the weeks turned into months, he settled in and eventually did make a couple of friends. They talked about the reasons they were all incarcerated, what they would eat first the minute they were released, and about a gal back home that they hoped would still be waiting for them, although most of them had doubts they would actually wait it out.

Thomas was the one inmate Ishmael connected with best. He was a born steel man like himself and had tales of fighting while intoxicated that sounded eerily similar to that of Ish's grand tales. Both men had trouble dropping the liquor from their diets but had learned to handle life without the hangovers better as time went on.

When he learned that Thomas had family in Wilmington, Delaware, an instant bond was forged. Both men had long roots in the country, and both had families that hailed from the same area. Thomas had four children, and a wife that was now living with family while Thomas handled his debt to society.

He was arrested for killing an armed man, and although he swore it was in self-defense, he was drunker than hell and fought with the police who tried to speak with him about the matter. When he hit one of them over the head with an empty whiskey bottle, that sealed his fate. Guilty of second-degree murder, same as Ish, but with a slightly longer sentence of four years owed. Ish felt that maybe he had been blessed to only been giving that two-and-a-half-year sentence instead of more. He was learning to find small, happy moments wherever he could, and could see that being positive went a longer way in recovery.

One thing Ish learned through this all was that it was high time to make some adjustments in his life. As he told his new friend Thomas about the way he had lived up until this moment, and his desire to forge a better future for what life he had left to live,

"If nothing changes, nothing changes."

Chapter 27

* * *

Back home, Grace was transitioning from place to place, just trying to find her way to something that resembled a stable life. She had heard that Amos had been asking about her, but she paid little mind as she knew her life without him was better than it had been with. Even though she seemed to be lost in place, she counted her blessings as best she could.

She, of course, knew that Ish was in prison, and while she could feel some sense that he deserved each day he was sentenced to for the life he had traveled, she also knew that he was a man who loved his grandchildren and his son very much, and she saw for the time apart as a tremendous loss for all of them. She had thought about writing to him with updates, but let that task go to Annie and William. She just did not want to open old wounds that had been healed with bitter scars.

Ishmael was getting by, but the first winter behind those walls was brutal. The cold air that encapsulated the prison grounds came off the water outside the walls of the penitentiary. He was used to working through the cold, but this was different, as the heat that came off the steel he worked with was of some comfort. The cold air sat there with seemingly no purpose, other than to torment the men who resided inside the dark walls and to remind them that they had done terrible things to end up here. Men were growing frustrated with little to nothing to do, and Ish could tell that things could easily get out of hand there.

The living conditions were not hospitable, as was expected, but as a man of his size, he felt cramped for the long hours spent behind the bars. Being outside to wander in the yard was the only welcoming side of braving the cold air.

Groups of men would find their way to particular sides of the grounds, but Ish, being a newer prisoner and not born of the area, seemed like an outcast. His size meant little to the incarcerated men there, and surely, he would be outnumbered if anything should happen and he lost his temper. On the outside, his lack of one leg did not hamper him much at all, because he usually only had to deal with a handful of brave souls, but inside here, it would be much different.

That first year went by painfully slow, and although he was growing used to the conditions and his surroundings, he was sorely regretting most of his life choices and began to write promises to himself on small pieces of notepaper to remind him that when he got out, he would never be coming back. This was going to be the wakeup call that he desperately needed, and he would settle for no less.

By the first summer there, he had avoided trouble with a few minor exceptions. There were the occasional tough guys who wanted to try the big man on for size, but mostly those moments came and went with not much of an issue other than a temper flare here and there. One thing Ish always did was to stand his ground. It helped that he had no fear of any man that God put on this earth, and that he was the type of person that would go out on his sword if that was what was needed.

In early June he received a letter from both his young William and Annie. She was pregnant again and their family was once again growing in numbers. This made Ish smile as he read the letter and gave him something to look forward to upon his release. William even told Ish that he felt this one was going to be a boy. When Ish wrote him back he said,

"William, I hope you are right. A healthy grandson would do just fine. Give him a name unlike mine, though. I want him not to have the curses which he cannot escape, and a name can do a lot for a man to deter his success."

By the end of the first year, in late December, just before the Christmas holiday, Carroll Francis Hill was born. Not only did he not have the given name of Ishmael, he also did not bear his last name. Sometime over the last decade, Grace had changed her name back to match that of her son's, William, but a census worker had made an error when he asked her for her full name. Her Irish brogue was thick, and when she said the name Heald, he heard it as Hill, which is what the name Heald generally means. So the name had changed for William then, but Ishmael never made or needed to make the same adjustment as he was not living there at the time.

Ish shared the news with Thomas and a few other inmates that he was locked in with, and although they could not toast to this, they imagined that they were on the outside, and each with a drink in hand, cheered the big man.

"Ish, it'll be here before you know it, and you will have that grandson of yours high in the air. You just hang on and you'll see," Thomas said.

He was growing impatient though as all he wanted to do was see his family and make up for the years of abuse he had dealt out to others and to his own body. Time had taken hold of Ish's mind as he sat there and he was forced to relive all those moments he would rather sooner forget.

There were many nights where Mary Agnes would invade his mind as he tried to sleep, and he would wake up to believe she was right there with him, just as she was before she passed away. But he was rudely aware that when his eyes opened, it was not to be.

The fight he had with Amos was one he would go back to many times on those long days alone in his cell, wondering if he should have finished the fight in death, so that he felt some type of honor in revenge for him for what happened to his little girl. Ish never came to terms with the fact he felt Amos had more to do with her leaving this life, and he frustrated himself wondering if he would have one more shot at that son-of-a-bitch. He would probably be getting out by now.

There were nights where he could see Henry as if he were right there with him in the cell. Ish would beg him to forgive him for the shooting over and over, and Henry, in his mind, would say not a word, but smile. Ish was unsure if this was his way of mercifully forgiving him, or perhaps the opposite, letting him know he was keenly aware of what was awaiting him on his death.

His mind wrestled with so many consequences of past actions, and they began to haunt his dreams nightly for months on end. All he wanted was peace from that past he had no more control over, but perhaps peace was not what he needed to move forward to a better life. So, he allowed those dreams to violate his mind as they saw fit.

In 1909, Ish had completed his first year at "The Wall," and was feeling more relaxed. Those horrifying moments of seeing others he had regrets over, had for the most part, passed on. He was now more focused on seeing the light ahead with just over a year left to his sentence.

His brother, William, had been writing to let him know about all the tales he was facing back in uniform in the town they grew up in. There were arrests at ball games where young boys were rumbling each other to express dominance and territorial rights as they saw fit. During one such incident, William was thrown to the bottom of the pile while in full uniform, holding on to two or three boys, while desperately trying to gain control. He told Ish,

"No one has any sort of respect for the colors I wear, and the badge I hold. It's as if the world is going mad and I am trying to remind it there are better things to do with your time, but my words seem to fall on deaf ears."

Ish laughed at those stories, but not because his brother was in danger of being hurt. He did so more because he remembered himself as a young kid doing just about the same. He knew boys would be boys, but even he was a little shocked at the sheer boldness of the new generation of youth.

It did remind him, however, of the time he beat a constable with a nailed board. Maybe these boys were not much different from him, and again, all he could do was smile, knowing his past was surely no different.

He figured that as long as no little, senile old ladies were shooting at William over stolen chickens, his brother was going to be alright. It's the life he had chosen, after all. Even if no one expected to have to duck for cover from those not meant to handle a gun.

In the middle of 1910, on a welcomed warm day, after spending close to one thousand days behind iron, steel, and gray colored blocks that could make a man go insane, Ishmael Heald was finally released back into the world. He was given back his collar buttons, the razor he had, and the twenty-five cents he had to his name when he first entered through the gates.

He walked to the entrance of the prison, looked back once before exiting to remind himself to never visit this place again, and without a word to anyone, walked out a free man, his debt paid in full.

He jumped onto a passenger train, heading back east to where he was from, and decided he needed to make one stop before going back to Conshohocken to be with his family. He needed to say one final goodbye to his friend, Henry, and to ask him for forgiveness, even if Henry could no longer grant that. It was just something he knew was right, and so he did.

There, Ish saw the stone with his friend's name, and the date of that fateful day that led to two-and-a-half years of his freedom being taken, although he somehow felt selfish for having been frustrated with his condition. It could be worse, he thought to himself. Look at young Henry. His sentence was permanent.

Chapter 28

Amos decided it was time to leave the area and search for new grounds in which to spend his time. He was told there was work in the town of Reading, Pennsylvania, and so right before Ish was released, he left by train and headed towards his new destination to secure work.

Not much had changed for him, though, as he was still heavily drinking and fighting almost everywhere he went. One of his daughters, Margaret, who was born from a marriage prior to Grace, was concerned for her father as he was clearly having issues with women more and more the older he got.

But the ladies enjoyed Amos when he wasn't causing life-threatening problems on others. He was able to convince them that he was a hard-working steel man, but with an inheritance on the way, any day now. Only, there was no such inheritance. His father was very much alive but had little to his own name to pass down to him.

He did this time and time again, and once his temper got the better of him and he lashed out with his usual rage and fury, he would simply move on and find someone else to con into a love affair.

Reading also seemed like a safer place for him. He knew Big Ish was now out of prison, and in the back of his mind, just as in Ish's mind, was the concern whether he would be pinned for what happened with Mary Agnes those years back. There were always rumors circulating that someone had overheard someone that was close to Ish, say that he was looking for him still to this day.

The truth was, however, that Ish was not. At least not yet. He was focused solely on those grandkids of his, and his family back in both Conshohocken and Norristown. Carroll was almost 2 years old, and Ish had yet to set eyes on the little guy. His freedom was important to him this time around.

After leaving the cemetery where he said a final goodbye to his friend, having asked for a little grace and forgiveness, Ish headed straight for home. He knew his brother would be awaiting his arrival, but when he started to see the town come into view just beyond the rolling hills, he could see just off to the left, his son, William, daughter-in-law, Annie, with a child in her arms, and a tiny little girl, all looking around excitedly.

"There, there he is Marion!" shouted William as he pointed in the direction of an aging man who came into view.

She was nervous at first, but knew that somehow, this

man was family. He got off the train, pushed past a few slower movers who were not in all that much of a rush, and picked her up into his arms. Nothing could have made this man happier than this very moment.

"Marion, just look at you. I bet you don't recall me much at all, but you will grow to know me once again," Ish stated.

He then held her in his arms, and walked over towards the others who were smiling.

"Dad, welcome home. It's great to see you," young William said.

William could see that the years had caught up with Ish, and although he stood as strong as ever, he had lines on his face that had never been there before. His hair was thinning some, and his stance was showing the pain from years of abusing it both physically and mentally.

Annie hugged Ish, telling him she hoped her handwritten letters had done some good in a place where very little good ever existed. Ish smiled and told her how much they kept his mind off of terrible things that he saw and dreamt about. But then he went right back to finding the good in this day so he could leave that time where he left it.

"And this little guy must be my newest grandson, Carroll," Ish exclaimed.

He had finally had the chance to have his small family back together, minus Grace of course, who had, in her mind, no business attending his return. This was not her place, and besides, she didn't care whether he was home or away in some concrete prison for the crimes he was accused of, or for those he had gotten away with over the decades. That was not of her concern any longer.

"Uncle William said he would see you at home. He wanted you to see the kids before you settled back in. Hope that's okay, Dad," William said.

But Ish hardly heard a word he spoke, for he was so involved in looking in the eyes of those tiny children, wondering how he had let life change his direction so terribly. He spoke softly to each, promising them a change in his ways, and letting them know they had their granddad back for good, cross his heart. He would never allow this to happen again.

Young William somehow believed that this time away, these two plus years of hell, had made such an impact on his father, that he could be telling the truth. This was the longest time he had been away, and as far as he could remember, going back years and decades before, the greatest distance between drinks he could recall his father having. When he wasn't on the whiskey, he looked and acted like an entirely different man.

The family eventually headed back into town, over to where William lived with his wife. They had a place in mind for Ish to rent on the main strip in town, but they knew he would need some time to secure work locally before he could rent a room. What they did know was that Ish was finished in Mifflin. There would be no more trips there, no matter how good the work was. He had been blessed enough to have survived a time when he could have easily been locked up for many more years than he was sentenced to. He had found a blessing in all that chaos.

Ish was a steel puddler and that was all he ever wanted to do, so he would secure work wherever he could, doing the art he called his for so many years. Puddling was becoming a thing of the past, as mills closed from the lack of needed steel production, and competition from further mills ate up the smaller local ones. But Conshohocken still had theirs, and Ish knew his reputation for being good at his trade was still intact.

"Mary, I see you are feeding old William well," laughed Ish.

Mary smiled, and William let out a laugh, realizing that he had indeed put some weight on since the last time his brother had seen him. William was doing well on the police force, and making a decent pay which allowed him to raise the kids and sock some away, just in case.

Ish, though, had very little to his name. If it weren't for family, he would be off anywhere but here, trying to secure work, while most likely stealing chickens and their eggs, just to survive until he could. He had remembered times when he would sneak into gardens of nearby houses, just to secure some sustenance for his body. Peppers, tomatoes, whatever a home was growing at the time, was fair game. There were some tough times for sure while he traveled around as a tramp.

"Ish, would you like a drink?" William offered, knowing his brother was probably waiting for such an offer after not having a drop while in the system.

But that was not the case. At least not for now. Ish wanted to continue on without his drinking for a while, just to see how much life could change when he was sober more often than not. He could feel the lost years behind him gone so quickly as they do, and the memories from those heavy drinking days were basically gone to him. He simply could not recall many at all, just as he could not recall when Henry was shot while in his shanty.

That was not a lie he told. He truly could not recall a lot of things in life, and felt that his fifty odd years had gone by in such a flash, that he had been cheated out of them. In those two and a half years, he had so much time to reflect on the what-ifs and what could have beens, that he was surprised he didn't go mad while inside "The Wall."

"Not today, William. I just want to eat a fine home-cooked meal, if Mary will allow, and stay in with you and the family. That would be the finest first night home I can imagine," he said.

William was surprised, but genuinely happy to hear that. He knew his brother had such a good heart when he was sober, and that when he was on that hell whiskey of his, he could not find peace. So for him to hear that Ish wanted no parts of it, at the very least for an evening home, he was pleased.

Once again, Ish was able to secure some work, but for now it was outside the steel work he was accustomed to. William knew of a man who needed someone who was both handy and hardworking, and he recommended his brother. At first, the man was not too pleased to oblige, but with a little reminding that having a cop friend had its perks, the man relented.

He was right, though. Ish worked hard and could fix anything his hands touched. Because he had curbed his drinking, he was more focused on what he was doing, versus what he wanted to be doing. He would wake up early in the morning and have a full memory of what happened the night before and could immediately get going for the day's work ahead.

After a few short months, Ish was able to secure boarding at that place on Fayette Street his brother had mentioned when he first arrived back home. It wasn't anything fancy, but it was well suited for his needs. Being a basic type of guy had its perks for certain at times.

After the remainder of 1910 went by, and after having proved his worth with those he knew, he was offered another crack at the thing he loved most. Ish became a puddler again, and nothing could make the man happier. This was simply what he was born to do.

So, life was back on track. With his son seemingly proud of his father, and those grand-babies growing to know the man they had lost, he just felt as if good times were ahead finally. Not knowing how long he had left was both a blessing and a curse, he thought.

But then being sober had its issues as well. His body was not what it once was, and he realized how much drinking had self-medicated him into getting through those nights following a physically taxing week. It also did not allow his mind to shut off, and there were days which he wished he could forget.

One such day, he was hanging out with some old friends from years ago. They were good men who worked at the plant, but heavy drinkers like Ish had once been. It started out with them reminiscing over the stories they had remembered, including many Ish had forgotten. Stories of drinking late into the dangers of the night, and those of fighting for the hell of it.

But a man named George brought up the ill-fated night when his daughter had passed. He meant no harm, but was instead curious if anyone ever stood accountable for what had happened.

It reminded Ish that when Henry had died, there was a sense of accountability with him having served the time deemed necessary. But when Mary Agnes passed away, it simply was not the same. The police had been convinced she had taken her own life in a moment of sadness so great she could not realize the joys to come. But there were those who thought otherwise. Even the newspapers had to question the investigation that had been carried out, in their words, terribly.

At the time, some felt she had been killed by the man in Wilmington as revenge for her testimony that almost destroyed his family and career. Others felt that a jealous man who may have wanted to court her, was to blame for the tragic poisoning of a young woman who found herself on the wrong side of life.

But Grace had always wondered if Amos Alexander had told the truth about what he recalled. Had he really witnessed a dapper dressed man speaking to her? With his temper and sense of control, it seemed a little far-fetched that he would simply back off and let this man have his time with her daughter alone. There were seldom times where Amos allowed a man time with her without his interjecting his jealousy in one way or another.

He had not spoken to Grace for many years, but he knew how she felt and how she at times took the burden of responsibility for having introduced them in the first place. Surely she was alone and Amos had used his charm to get Grace's attention, but she knew better. She could see the way he talked with Mary Agnes and the way he tried to protect her from any man who would give her the slightest of attention.

It was not as a father would do, but more as a jealous lover, and she had either missed that, or wanted to believe it was not something possible. This was her husband and the man she was there to support, care for, and love. Nothing more. Although after the fact, it did feel like more.

When George reminded Ish that there was basically still someone out there who knew more, it sent him into a brief state of anxiety. He, as a father, had a duty to own revenge on whomever had a hand in this, and though he could recall the time he beat him from within a few inches of life, he had never felt satisfied with allowing Amos to continue breathing, when someone he had loved was unable to.

He sat there, listening to these men talk over drinks, recalling times that if he had a choice, he would close off his mind in a vault and lose the combination, even if it meant forgetting some of the good times. Some pain was not worth the happy moments that accompanied them, he thought to himself. But he had no choice in what his mind wanted him to recall. Especially when it would race at night through memory after memory, without his approval or request.

He felt as if he was back in a prison cell, unable to escape his own thoughts, and that the penance for having committed a terrible crime was to relive that night over and over until he could come to terms with what had truly happened.

Here, even though he had nothing to do with his daughter's passing, he felt that same penance was due. Maybe it was out of regret for not having the bond with her that he had with young William. What if it were because he was away, knowing fully well that a daughter needed a father to stand by just in case, and he was far off, not able to be that man. Whatever it was, his guilt was raging a powerful storm that no matter where he went in his head, he could not escape.

Some storms were there to remind you of unfinished business, and despite your strongest desires to leave those terrible memories in a time that you thought was clearly gone, you were forced to be reminded that perhaps they weren't. And a struggle ensued from within that you were not going to easily escape, so you had to make a decision to either accept your fate of having to deal with those nightmare moments or figure out a way to get revenge that would, hopefully, end those years and miles of regret.

As the year was coming to a close, Ish started to pick up the bottle again, claiming that his body and mind both needed a break from reality. He swore it was just temporary, but he knew better. As much as he had enjoyed being away from it, he had needed it more than that break.

The following year was going to bring change to the family once again, that would affect many. It would be a reminder that life was both fragile and quick, and that memories had a purpose. The life to come and the life to pass were both fragile, and both came and left as a part of this journey. One brought happiness, and the other, usually regret.

And so it would happen.

Chapter 29

The Summer the following year, 1911, Grace was hospitalized, having complained over more than a months' time that her heart was giving her an uncomfortable sensation. At the same time, Annie was with issue, ready to give birth at any time to her fourth child, and hopefully her third surviving.

It was a lot on young William to have excitement and fear at the same time, but he knew Grace had handled so many other terrifying times, that this, too, she would get through.

Only, it was not to be for her this time around. On August 20th, 1911, after having been hospitalized for nearly a month and with no real improvement, Grace Waters Hill, took her final breath. A woman who had lived a life of absolute struggle and regret through some of the toughest moments in life, but had found a bit of true happiness in the smallest of moments, passed on to be with her daughter Mary Agnes.

She had spent several days speaking to William about

what she wanted to do when she was able to get back home, but she was also keenly aware she may not leave the hospital alive. So, she used some of that time to ask for any forgiveness she needed to, even though William never held anything against her. She was a good grandmother, and while they had their differences as mother and son, he was still ultimately proud of the woman she was despite the tragedy that had dominated her lifetime

Young William went home and told Annie about the death of his mother, and began to plan for her burial. He knew that as much as Ish and she fought, he would want to know that his first love, first wife, and the woman with whom he had a child that had died too soon, had moved on to head back home to be with God.

Ish sat back and took a deep sigh through his nose.

"I'm genuinely sorry for your loss, William. She was a tough gal, no doubt about that, but I know her heart was in the right place most times. I'm just sorry to have not said goodbye," Ish said.

He was sincere in his words, because as he aged, Ishmael understood that life could and would end eventually, most likely without his say-so, and possibly without a moment to say a final goodbye. He was at least happy that Grace had a moment to be with her son, but somehow saddened that she had not mentioned his name.

It all gave Ish pause, knowing that he could have been better to that woman at times, but had ultimately decided against it for whatever reason. Most likely it was the liquor he had consumed over the decades of his own difficult life that had spurred those bad decisions. It left him mostly a different man than he intended, and the drink decided what he was incapable of.

Grace was buried a few days later in Saint Patrick's Cemetery in the town of Norristown, Pennsylvania. She was at rest, and no longer needed to deal with the pains and troubles that life had subjected her to. She had finally found her peace.

Within a month's time, the birth of Elizabeth Anna Hill was announced, and life was about getting back to loving, allowing grieving to be a memory. Old Ishmael had told his grandson William once,

"You spend a moment in time saying goodbye, but be sure you don't stay in that moment for any longer than you need, boy. God intended for you to look forward, and not behind. It's perfectly fine to miss something or someone, but not to miss out on something or someone to come."

It made perfect sense for young William. He knew what his grandfather meant. If he stayed lost in a difficult or sad moment, he would miss out on the chance to enjoy all the joys of life that came with watching young children grow up. It went fast when you looked back, so he tried to enjoy each sound and monumental moment the children had, from their first crawl to the first words they spoke. It was a blessing to have a chance to parent and he knew that.

As winter came, the demand for steel workers was picking back up. Ish found himself traveling for weeks at a time to different parts of the state, hoping to mostly stay out of trouble, but more so to stay unnoticed. He was aging, and by this point in life, preferred to stay out of the limelight.

His drinking wasn't as bad as it once was, but he surely wasn't able to remove it from his diet all together. There were some things he felt he could not control, and this would be one of them; he would just accept it.

But that all would only last so long, as on a trip to the Reading area for some work, Ish was short-tempered and aware that Amos was in the same area as him. On a train platform, another worker was frustrated with the pace at which Ish was getting off the train, and began to belittle the aging, but still larger man with the gimp leg.

"Old timer, you have any other speed at which you can move yourself?" he said.

At first, Ish tried to ignore the fool of a man, fearing that after a long prison sentence, another infraction could land him right back to where he came from. He just acted as if he had not heard the man, and continued on his way off the platform.

But the man, more frustrated at being ignored, continued to push at Ish, realizing that his much younger age gave him a clear advantage, or so he thought.

He grabbed at the overcoat Ish had on with one hand, and smacked the hat off his head with the other, unaware that he was waking a sleeping giant.

As Ish turned around, the red in his eyes gave notice to this kid that he had made a grave mistake. He was clearly angered, and now felt that he once again needed to remind others that there are men you can play with, and then there are men, that once you mess with, you look back on in ten years' time and still never get over the regret of your decision.

He grabbed at the man's throat, lifted him clear off the ground by what witnesses said was a good six inches or more, and pulled him into his personal space. The man, quickly started to apologize, saying that he was only messing around and meant no harm at all, shook with a great fear. He began to beg Ish to put his feet back onto the ground and let him be.

Ish, luckily, was able to slow his mind, for if he had not, this man would have lived that regretting ten years for certain, and they both knew it.

The man's feet dangled feverishly off the ground for what seemed like minutes, trying desperately to reach back to earth to ease the pain caused by the giant of a man who was in absolute control of that entire moment. Nothing, not even begging, could get this man to drop him without his say so.

Eventually, Ish regained his composure, and at a good time. There was a police man who had noticed a small crowd gathering nearby and was on his way to see what the commotion was about.

Ish had placed the man back down, smacked him in the head with those large, strong-as-steel hands, and knocked some sense into the youngin.

"Be careful of the man you think is beneath you, son.

For you have not a clue as to what he has had to endure and fight through in order to be right here, at this very moment, in this exact spot I now stand," Ish said.

The man saw the officer close, but decided to accept this as a lesson, rather than trying to have the big guy arrested. He knew that if he had, the chance of him being arrested at the same time was probable, and he could ill afford to spend time behind bars, especially if the same man who had just manhandled him with such ease was behind those bars.

The crowd that formed moments ago, realizing it was over, disbursed, and then the man whom Ish had nearly scared the very life from, walked in the complete opposite direction from the officer, forgetting if he was coming or going.

"Everything alright over here, fella?" the officer asked with a sense of entitlement.

Ish looked towards the man walking away confused, and without turning in the officer's direction, said,

"It is perfectly fine. Just a lesson in life for a young man who could use one, nothing more."

The officer looked Ish up and down, with a dead serious look in his eyes, before cracking a slight smile and responding back,

"This youth has not a clue as to what we have seen. I'm assuming you got your point across to the young lad, and there won't be any trouble from it all, am I right?"

Ish finally smiled back and nodded.

"You have assumed right. The message was received clear as day," he replied.

Amos was working at a different location, and Ish was aware now. So he should be good to not run into him, and he swore to himself this was just a temporary stop. He could avoid the dumb luck of running into Amos if he stayed clear of the bars the steel men enjoyed after long hours.

Part of him felt disappointed that Grace had passed earlier, and he wondered if the life both he and Amos had bestowed upon Grace had anything to do with her passing at a younger age than expected. He could not forgive himself for his role, but Amos, he had more trouble forgiving. The death of a daughter, and the death of an ex-wife, whom he at one time loved, troubled Ish. He always had in the back of his mind that had he stepped up long ago to this man, maybe life would be different for those women in his life.

Perhaps his daughter would still be alive, with a growing family of her own, and a much better life ahead of her. Maybe his own father, Ishmael Sr, would have lived for several more years, ensuring those words of wisdom he spoke at the most opportune times continued to land on the ears of those in need of them most. Grace may still be very much alive for her grandchildren, and even though they would never be together again and she would still hate the man's guts, Ish would not feel terrible about her death.

But this man, Amos Alexander, has caused so much turmoil in Big Ish's life, that he wondered if he would ever live a day without wanting to send him to his maker, or better yet, to the devil himself. He had lived a life causing both pain and destruction and would be a perfect candidate to spend eternity suffering the flames of hell.

After a few months, Ish would be called back to the Norristown area, and to his next assignment. He was all too pleased to be heading home, for it allowed him to be closer to his growing family, and removed him from spending each waking minute wondering if and when he would run into Amos. He knew that if he did, he would quite possibly spend the remainder of his days locked in a cage with the only way out in a pine box buried beneath the prison's grounds.

Back home, he seemed to be in a better element for himself and swore to his son that he would once again attempt to swear off the liquor, but he knew it would be a difficult task. After two plus years of not having a drop, it pained him to know he had once again slipped back into a habit that seemed both a necessity and a drain on what life he had left to go.

William made him promise that if he had more than a few, he would refrain from visiting the grandkids, as his speech and manners while on the drink were starting to grow more out of hand. This was usually only the case when he was dealing with steel men or other tramps he had encountered along his journey, but now it was including the people he loved most.

For her part, Annie felt genuinely bad for Ish, knowing his heart was as large as he was, but that he just could not catch a break in life. He was destined to struggle throughout the remainder of his days, and most likely would need to work until the very end, and she felt that was no life for a decent human to have to endure.

But she also knew he had made such terrible choices as a young man and had really no one to blame but himself. Still, though, she was possibly the most kind-hearted human that Ish had ever come into contact with, and she would always see to it that he had family somewhere.

Even on the days when in his mind he had not had more than his share to drink, but others would feel differently, she would ask him to sit on the porch and wait. She would bring him out a sandwich and a cold glass of water, hoping to soak up some of the alcohol from his system. Sometimes it would seemingly work, while others, she would just need to tell William that when he was by, he was mostly fine.

The grandkids couldn't care less about their grandfather's condition. They loved it when Paw-Paw Ish would stop by and hand a piece of candy to them, or if work was a busy week, perhaps a small toy they could share amongst themselves. They were simply children and loved, without needing to know what was expected of this man.

As the year went on, William had to face the fact that his father was just not capable of a full reform. This was the man he was, and you could accept that, or not. Those were his only options. With his mother now buried beneath the soil, he decided that he would just love his old man for all he wanted to be.

Ish struggled, knowing he was failing his son over and

over, but damnit if he could do this on his own. His son knew nothing of the work and life Ish had felt, the loss of a limb, and the pain of breaking a man's face with his bare hands, until he could no longer hit with them. He had broken his nose more times than he could remember and had scars throughout his aging body from working with steel, being hit by a bottle over his head, and who knows what else.

The struggle that a man endured such as that was often misunderstood, and as times changed, and the world came to different terms with how people should be treated, he could only wish it would have changed much sooner. Perhaps his worn-down, weathered body would not need so much self-medicating.

Chapter 30

* * *

Another year had come, and another year had gone, but the pace with which the years went by seemed to have picked up a decent head of steam. Grace was missed terribly by her family, but they knew it was time to focus on what was still to come, for the life they had left to live seemed worth living.

William, Ish's brother, was thriving in his career. There were a few times during their visits where he would listen to Ish speak of the steel plants and how the men who worked them would bond over the commonness of it all, especially those who resided together in makeshift living quarters most others would find unfit. William would wonder where he would be now had he not joined the force and instead, continued on beating his body down with the grueling repetition.

But thankfully, as much as he enjoyed physical work, as the Heald family came from a long line of a strong, able-bodied men, his body was all the better for not having

221

to handle the rigorous grind of that of a steely, as they were often called by others.

He was well known in his hometown, and well respected both there and in the surrounding communities that bordered Conshohocken. He was fair, and ultimately tried to give others the benefit of the doubt when they were accused of a crime. It probably had something to do with watching his own brother arrested dozens of times over his life, and him feeling a bit guilty that his own life was not the same. They were truly as different as iron was to that of red clay, but at the end of it, they were blood, and that to William meant everything.

Mary Heald, his wife, was also truly respected by the members of the community. She was a member of many local groups and enjoyed the five grandchildren they now had. Life was good for them, and their marriage had tested the times and survived. People would often say of the couple,

> "If there ever were two souls meant to be tied together through eternity, it would be them."

William was extremely patient despite the dealings he had to handle, and the dumb criminals that would test stupidity to new levels that would even shock a seasoned officer like himself.

The last winter was a little rough on Mary, who started to come down with more illness than she was used to, but there was a lot going around, and rumors had spread of a nationally notifiable disease, known as the measles. It kept people wondering what could be next, but as they always had, they persevered.

"Ish, you been down to see Mary Agnes yet this year?" William asked.

William had stopped down a few times on his own, but really hadn't talked with his brother about it much as of late. There was a lot else going on, and truthfully when Ish was in prison, everyone was just glad to have him back with the family upon his release. So the conversation never came up.

Ish just looked away, almost embarrassed to testify that he had not. In fact, he had tried desperately to put the past behind him so that he could let that pain and anger from that part of his life dissipate. He would never forget who she was or just what had happened to her, but what was the point of heading out to talk with a stone that would never speak back, and what would it do but further anger a man who was just trying to finish out his days, whatever ones were going to be granted to him?

Grace had passed away and if you asked Ish, she should have had plenty of extra days to roam this place with her ever-growing bundle of grandbabies. He remembered what it was like when they met, and how difficult times were for the two of them.

Honestly, he was angered that he had not provided a much better life for her, and that he quickly drove her away with his practice of liquor consumption, which allowed his temper to be on full display for anyone within arm's reach, and in turn, chased freedom from him with each mistake he made. He had never properly made an attempt to be a good provider, which she and those two children needed.

So here he was, trying to let a past stay much where it should, while the lessons, obvious for certain, clearing a man's heart of all it should have cherished. He would be damned if he didn't at least give life one last go before his sand ran out.

Ish used all his free time to find reasons to not enjoy the pleasures of a drink, but could find few. His friends were moving on, starting families of their own, or traveling away to mills that were searching for strong, young and able-bodied men to continue their growth. What he had left was a son whom he bonded with here and there over the decades, some grandbabies that seemed to accept this man for exactly what he was, and a brother that always told him how proud he was, but he knew that pride could not be granted truthfully to a man who had failed so many times for little reason.

Because William worked such long shifts, Ish would stop on by to check on Mary throughout the year he was back home, making sure she was okay. She had always done right by him, judging not as the man she saw, but instead, judging as the man he wished he could have been. She was always finding the best in someone, even a tramp like him.

In late November of that year, though, Mary started to show signs that she was having further difficulty shaking this nonsense cold of hers, and William confided in Ish that he was worried just a little more than he expected to be, even with Mary's assurance of,

"Nonsense, William. I am finer than I've ever been. This is nothing more than a reminder to slow down for most, but I know of no such thing," she would say smiling.

William knew a thing or two about refusing to slow to the times. He would work himself every waking hour available, just so he could both get ahead, and ensure his town that he loved almost as much as life itself, was the better for it.

But as the start of December had come, Mary was diagnosed with tuberculosis, and to everyone's surprise, within only a week and a half, she no longer had that Irish fight within, and on December 10th, at exactly three in the afternoon, she passed away, leaving William a widower after having been married for the better part of 32 years, of which each one seemed better than the last.

Apparently, she had known more about her sickness than she let on. She did not want William to worry about her, because he simply had enough to worry about in his daily duties. She would pull through, she reckoned, and it would not make a hill of beans of difference. She simply did not expect to lose the battle, and never felt the need to tell anyone until there was no way around it.

William had the task of preparing her wake, and met

with the undertaker to arrange sending his wife off. It was attended by many of the town folk and held at the home of William and Mary. It would be the last time the two of them were together in the home they had lovingly made theirs.

Mary was to be buried at Saint Matthew's Cemetery, which was just a short walk from where she had spent many years raising her children and loving her husband. She was, as William would say, the foundation of their beautiful family and the reason he had done as well as he had.

Ish knew William was in pain, although if anyone could hide it, it was him. He was told to take the rest of the week off from work, but he would hear none of that.

"The wrongdoers do not take a break for things of this nature, so I must do as needed. Mary would have insisted," he said.

It was a devastating time for William and his children, who relied on Mary for many things in life, including keeping order from within, as most families need. She would be missed, and William, well, William knew life was never going to be the same.

Ish gave his brother time as he knew no words he could muster up would be on any consolation. In times such as these, sometimes you must allow a man to find his own words in his own time and in his own way, as strong men often had to do.

Loss of course was nothing new to the Heald family, as they, over the generations that had long passed, learned to continue on through many difficult moments. Ish had known loss clearly, but even he knew that the loss of a wife who refused to allow her aliments to interfere with the man she loved, was greater than anything he could possibly imagine. After all, his daughter had been estranged for some time, and despite him once loving Grace, it had been long since she had been any part of his daily routine.

A few weeks had passed, and another officer who worked with William over at the police department came in to find William one evening.

"I was hoping you were here. There's a disturbance and, well, you better come and see," he said.

William was filling out some paperwork, nearly complete with the shift that had kept him away from home for well over eleven hours and was fitting to head home for a deserved rest.

Rather than ask the officer what the commotion was, William decided to simply head out and follow his partner, figuring he would know soon enough what was going on. Besides, an extra hour was not going to change much for him, as he seldom enjoyed being at home without Mary there. It felt empty and cold being there alone. He felt selfish for having not died alongside his wife.

When they arrived a few blocks away, there were two men sitting on the ground, both drunker than hell, and bloodied from what appeared to be a heck of a fight. When William got within sight, he could clearly see the reason for him being summoned at the end of his day.

"Ish, by God what are you doing?" he demanded.

But Big Ish was so inebriated, he had not even known William was in his presence. He was just saying nonsense about nothing much, cussing at the other man, who seemed worse off than Ish. The other man was lumped up with bruises about his cheek and jawline, and surely in some pain that the alcohol in his system was probably keeping manageable.

William didn't hesitate, telling the other officer to lock them both up, and let the judge deal with them in the morning. When the officer looked at William to make sure he had heard him right, William, in an uncharacteristic way, said,

"Well what are you waiting on? You heard me right. Damnit I don't need this tonight."

The following morning, Big Ish was sober enough to realize he had some trouble the night before. His large hands ached and his wooden leg that supported the leg he had lost many years ago, was nearly broken in two. His head hurt something awful, and the other man who had been involved with him, was still sleeping it all off.

Ish grabbed at the top of his head, and tried to figure out both where he was and why he was there. From experience, he knew he had done wrong, and that more than likely someone was hurting worse than he, and there would be a court involved once again. Nothing seemed to change, and he was both confused and frustrated with himself.

Within an hour, there was William, walking in for the day's work, unsure of what he should do with Ish and this other man. On one hand, he wanted to cut his brother free and allow him to correct his misdoings as family often forgave family, but on the other hand, he knew they were never corrected. Ish had trouble with the whiskey, and that sadly was just never going to change. The few years he spent away from the demons had not helped him nearly enough, despite good intentions.

"William, I'm sorry. I know I let you down, and with all you are dealing with…"

but William cut him off before he could finish.

"Why? Why cannot you see just what you have done over and over? Why is it you cannot understand that this is no way for any man to travel in life? Do you not care for anyone but yourself? Is that the problem?" William asked angrily.

Now Ish felt terrible, and embarrassed at the same time. He had always admired his brother, and here he was, laying into him at the police station, where one brother was on each side of the bars. Both had come from the same parents, and from the very same town down in Delaware. Both had moved here at the exact same time, living in the neighborhood the other roamed in. Even the jobs they held at the same times, were nearly identical. But that is where the similarities ended. They were so far apart at this very moment that if you did not know they were brothers, you would think them to be nothing alike.

For being born under the same circumstances had not allowed them to be two of a kind. They were as different as black was to white, and although they both had good hearts deep down, only one could convince others of that.

He knew, he had made an error in judgement once again, but in his defense, he felt at least he could not remember a single detail other than he had started drinking early in the day, feeling as if his demons were messing with his mind a little more than he would have liked.

From there, things got foggy and the next thing he knew, he was waking up and looking at his brother on the other side. The blacking out was nothing new to him, and it was clearly apparent to William, this was something you either accepted in someone, or moved on from. He knew not what to do, and without Mary there to remind him that family is always welcomed and always forgiven, he would need time.

He told the other officer to open the cell, wake up the other fella, and release them both. He had not the time nor the patience to see them through a hearing with a judge, and honestly, he did not want to bring shame to his family's name again. Besides, what was the judge really going to do for the crime of fighting while intoxicated? It happened nearly every hour on some street in the borough as darkness crept in. It would simply be a waste of everyone's time.

"Go home Ish. Get some rest, and see your grandbabies. Just get out of town for a little. I need a break," William said.

Ish did as William demanded, and headed back into Norristown to visit with young William and Annie. He would do as told and stay there for a few weeks, if they would allow, until he could find a new place and area to stay. All he needed was a little time to get himself together, he continued to tell himself. But no matter how many times he told himself this, there never seemed to be that time.

And he felt as if he embarrassed his brother. For that, he was truly remorseful.

Chapter 31

* * *

The steel world was starting to experience a resurgence by the time the year 1913 rolled in, and men of skill, especially puddlers, were in extremely high demand for their dying skills. There were few who understood the art of the trade, and who were strong and dedicated enough to handle such a job.

Ish was getting offers from mills all over the eastern side of the country, including as far as Ohio. He started to take jobs that would last a few months at a time, often showing younger men just how he had made a living with his craft over the decades he had under his belt.

The hard part was that it was physically different from what a lot of men were accustomed to, but being built for such a job, made it seem simple for Ish and the men he worked side by side with. The life expectancy of a puddler, due to the strenuous labor, the extreme heat in the conditions they worked in, as well as the fumes associated with such work, was roughly no more than 30 years.

He was not the best at training younger men as he did not have the patience required for being an effective teacher, but what he did bring was a strong enough work ethic, so that if you watched the man at work, you could pick up just enough to be decent.

And young William? He was building that family of his, for what seemed like a yearly tradition. Annie was carrying once again, and due in the mid-fall of that year. They had a healthy love, and being that she was Irish Catholic, having babies seemed more of a duty than anything else.

Ishmael had traveled out to Lancaster again, a place he was very familiar with, but was hesitant to travel much further west. He knew that men in these mills had heard the story of the big drunk fool who shot a friend in what may have been an accident, or perhaps during a fit of rage. The story changed, depending on who told it and what one believed. Either way, he was truly looking to mind his business, stay low, and just work, and work hard.

He spoke with his brother here and there, but it seemed the strong brotherly bond had been possibly tested one too many times. Ish knew that when Mary passed, his brother needed a distraction, but not the kind he seemed to con-stantly provide. But he wondered when William would feel healed enough to sit with Ish as they once did, and just accept that he was the way he was and that was that.

In October, Annie delivered a baby boy, and they decided on the name Lawrence. Annie felt it sounded like roy-alty, and figured if she gave him a strong name meant for something purposeful in life, it could truly happen for him.

Ish was happy, but felt a deep void in his heart. His son was so busy working and taking care of those babies, that he seldom had time to hang out with his father. His brother was feeling lost in his life as well, and Ish thought it would be a great time for the two of them to lean on each other. Both had come through great losses in their time and could understand the other as a result.

But time was needed still, so Ish decided to take a job offer out in Youngstown, Ohio. They were short on experienced men, and when a representative of the mills out there came to town looking for men with experience, he jumped at the chance.

The pay was seven dollars per ton of puddling, more than Ish had ever made in his life. They had hired men from the Pottstown area, Reading area, and finally the Conshohocken area. All three areas were rich in men with experience, so naturally, they were hotspots for the representative to lure the best of the men.

Ish said his goodbyes, and wished everyone well. He said he would be back when he could, but being further out, and having to work as many hours as humanly possible to earn as much of that money they were paying, he was unsure of when that would be.

He did not say a goodbye to his brother, instead asking his son to mention to him that he had gone west, and would hopefully see him upon his return. Ish hoped that this break away, and hopefully a clean record while away, would help his brother realize that he was truly sorry for having caused an issue at all.

The trouble, though, was that there were several men from Reading who were also making the journey west, and that included Amos Alexander. Ish was not made aware until they joined the groups of men at the Norristown train terminal.

Immediately, the tension could be felt between the two men, but no one could figure out why. Most just thought it was a territorial thing between steel men from rival towns, and paid it little mind. It had, after all, been fourteen years since the passing of Mary Agnes. Most people had forgotten or had never heard of her tragic loss, but for a father, he never would forget.

The ride felt longer than it was for those two, and Ish decided to stay as far from that man as possible, fearing that a lost temper would cause his employment and more money than he had ever earned to quickly vanish. It would not be an easy task, but as Ish had always said, he did not wish to go back to prison for something he could not be fully certain of.

Amos, having realized so much time had passed, didn't have the fear he once did. He figured that Ish had aged, and with so many years gone, had lost that desire to send him straight to hell as he had once promised.

The first few weeks there were like most others for the men. You were shown your living quarters, which were not much different from what Ish had experienced in Shanty

Row, and led to the men in charge. Those men were strict, but eager to have experienced men there to help with the backup they were facing. To them, these men were a Godsend.

After everyone settled in when they arrived in Ohio, Ish mostly stuck to himself. He was afraid to meet men that would both become friends and drinking companions. He decided that on this trip, he would stand solo for as long as possible and avoid the pitfalls that had cursed him in the past. The hope was to serve out his time at the mill, save enough money to return home, find a new place of his own, and eventually, not need to put his body through the extreme treatment that being a puddler did. He needed some rest.

The days were once again draining, but as always, he kept up with everyone who was hired to help. If there was one thing Big Ish was known for, it was never to let anyone out work him. You could be two decades his junior, and you would have the hardest of times keeping pace with the old man.

That time went by much faster than expected, and a welcomed surprise for Ishmael was that Amos had gone back home to the Reading area, rumored to have been chased out by a few married men whose wives told of inappropriate advances by the man.

His reputation seemed to follow him wherever he traveled, and for that, Ish was smiling. He just did not need the distraction of Amos being so close that he could smell the terribleness off of him. Jail had not been a welcome home for those years, and if Ish had his way with Amos without the benefit of his brother stepping in to ensure he did not finish him off this time, he would possibly die behind bars.

Back home, William was noticeably working more hours on the force, patrolling the streets from early morning, until sometimes, late in the evening. He had always worked hard, but now seemed to need the work. It wasn't about the money, but more about the distraction for him.

He did take time to enjoy his children and their families, opting to use Sundays to gather as many together as he could. That, as he said it, was both the Lord's Day, and Mary's dying wish. He respected both greatly.

But he did miss talking with Ish. He had not heard from him since his brother had left for Youngstown, and wondered how he was doing. Even young William had heard very little about how his dad was doing. Ish had seemingly disappeared from their lives.

When the holidays came, there was no word. As the beginning of the next year came, it was more of the same. Both his brother and son began to worry. Men who worked at the mills could easily pass away from heart issues, or from accidents that happened more often than they did not.

It got to the point that William had made some inquiries within his police force, asking if they knew anyone close to the Youngstown plant. He would try to get word out as far across the state as possible, hoping to continue on with the chain that would eventually land on someone near where Ish was last known to have gone.

Throughout 1914, there was no word at all. Men had come back and more had gone out, but there was little word about Ish. He was thought to have been spotted by a few, but they could not be certain as the workload was tremendous, and they had little time to focus on much else. Even for a man who had stood out amongst all men his entire life, he had either blended in so well that he had accomplished his goal of being virtually invisible, or something bad had happened to him, and no one had been able to identify who the man was.

William had figured that maybe he ought to take some time from work and make the trip to Youngstown to investigate a little further. Because he was a member of law enforcement, he could make his way up the ladder a bit more, and possibly find out if there were any unsolved cases in the area. With a man of his size, and having been missing a leg for much of his adult life, things would stand out in the memory of someone, had they seen anyone who fit that description.

Even his son had contemplated going with Uncle William to offer a hand, but Annie needed him there. Things were financially tight as they were, and time off of work would mean time away from pay. They had just finally been able to make some ends meet, and this would set them back. Uncle William assured him that if he went out, he would either bring him home dead or alive, or prove that Ish was still very much alive and just working so much that he simply lost track of time.

In August of that year, without warning, and with William making the arrangements for the trip west, there came a man walking off the train station, with a hat covering the top of his head and slightly dipped over his eyes. He was large, walked with a slight limp, but stood proud above everyone around. He was clean, had a pleasant smile, and greeted folks that passed him by. As he continued down the streets of Conshohocken, down the main road, and to the avenues that housed so many of the town's hardest working people, he stopped in front of officer Heald's home.

With a hardy knock on the front door to announce his arrival, the man waited for William to open the door, and when he finally had, wondering just who it was this early on a Saturday morning, he saw standing there his brother, Big Ish, looking older than he had before, but still for the better. He was not his usual staggering self, but instead stood tall and proud as any man William had seen.

"Ishmael? Where the hell have you been? We've all been worried something awful," William said.

Ish stood there for a moment, then reached out his hand to grasp his brother's, and shook it with intent.

"I had some things to do in life, and that is what I did. I remember something I was told at a low moment in my life,

"If nothing changes, nothing changes." He said.

William invited him in and they sat down in the same spots they had back when Ish was being accused of murdering that man out in Mifflin. It was a familiar moment, except for the fact that Ish was no longer in fear of going to prison, and well, Mary was not there to make sure the brothers had what they needed before speaking in private.

Things had certainly changed, but the feeling of that room was just as it always was. Ish felt completely safe in the front room of that house, and knew, despite the time he and William had away from each other, that nothing could destroy the bond they had.

The two men sat down over coffee and discussed what was going on in their lives since they last spoke. William talked of missing his wife deeply, but that he had come to grips with the new life he had in front of him. He would, as he put it, miss the hell out of that little darling, but he also knew that he would be with her eventually, when the good God called him home.

Ish mentioned seeing Amos on the journey to Youngstown, but that he had somehow kept his cool well enough to fend off the demons that whispered to him to kill the son-of-a-bitch. He spoke of long, grueling days, and how he found a way to stay off the drink for almost the entire stay. He watched as men stumbled around the camps, looking like complete idiots, and he realized he would no longer participate as such.

There were also severe accidents at the mill. Mostly due to overworked men, who were fighting to stay awake during long hours of work, and seemingly longer hours of drinking during the little downtime they had. One fella, he said, had hot metal spill onto the lower part of his body, and with little time to react, had his legs removed by a doctor nearby.

He had watched as young men fought for no other reason than to prove something to everyone around, but Ish said he realized he had nothing to prove to anyone but himself. That that is what he did. He had shown himself that if he wanted change, he would need to change.

William sat in amazement as his brother spoke of his time away and of how he had done what no one felt he could. The lines in his face were carved deeper and could almost tell their own stories of struggle, but for this moment, William remembered his brother as a young boy, right before his first arrest at a young age for fighting. He wondered if things could have been different for Ish if he had wanted that long ago, or if this was just the right time for him to correct things.

Whatever the case, the men spoke for hours on end. William mentioned he was on his way out to check on things, which caught Ishmael off guard. He had no idea they even had a concern for him at all. When he last left, things were very different. But he could see that he was still loved for the man he was.

The money he had earned was good, and Ish told William he wanted to rent a place of his own, outside of the immediate area, to give himself a fresh start. He wanted to be a simple man, without the past that seemed to follow and haunt him wherever he went.

Life was simple for the two men for the first time in a good while. But simple was exactly what each man needed and deserved.

Chapter 32

* * *

With his money saved instead of being thrown at the devil's juice for self-medicating purposes, Ish was able to secure himself a place just on the outskirts of Harrisburg, which happened to be close to where he first went when leaving Mifflin after the horrific shooting.

He could easily make it back home to visit with family by way of train, but have that time away that was becoming more important to a man who always seemed to find the center of attention in any situation. At this point, he was a man of over fifty years, and drinking to the point of passing out, with the probability of fighting someone and hitting bone against bone to see which one broke first, was no longer something he found to be a good time.

He had also hurt his family in the process along the way. They had experienced anger towards him at times, and worse off, embarrassment. That was harder on him than anything else could be. He never wished for anyone to feel embarrassed to know him. That was where he missed his sister-in-law Mary most. She appeared to never judge anything he did, or didn't do, and he respected her tremendously for that. For if she did feel any sort of negativity towards him, she would never allow that to show.

He had once again stopped his drinking, and instead, had worked hard and steadily for this moment. It was a chance to show his family he was responsible, no longer just some tramp on the run, and had been strong enough to put the drinking in his past, which no one, including him, thought was a real possibility.

When most of his friends in the steel world were dying or had already passed on, he, for some odd reason, was still very much alive. It had not made a lot of sense to him, but he was grateful for the chance. Maybe he was destined to do something great before his time expired, but he was not certain about that.

He looked around at the humble place he was renting and called home, and smiled as he sat down in an old chair that William had given to him. He had very little to his name, but what he had was a gift. The landlord of the property had also left some items that Ish was able to use. But his most prized possession, the one thing he treasured more than anything on earth, was a pair of shoes that Mary Agnes had worn as a small child. He kept them at his son's house while he was traveling to different cities for work over the years, but now that he had a place to call his, he wanted them close to him.

Whenever he was feeling particularly down about things, he would go back to a memory that pleased him, those of Grace giving birth to the children and the first time he was able to hold them. A time when Grace had not hated him for his worthlessness and they smiled together, although rare, it was memorable enough still. Those grandbabies he had and cherished more than even his own kids and the joy they had when he brought them the simplest of gifts.

In August of 1915, Ish was at home after a day's work, resting and reading from a book he had been gifted a few weeks back. He was seated in his kitchen, at just about seven in the evening, when he decided to light the lamp in the kitchen for some light. Just about thirty minutes later, he noticed the lamp was running low on oil, but he was still not ready to shut things down for the evening.

He grabbed the can of kerosene he had purchased early in the day, and went over to the lamp so that he could fill it for the remainder of the evening. He was so focused on reading, that he forgot to close the flame down to be safe. Instead, he attempted to fill the lamp while the flame was still very much alive.

In an instant, the oil caught fire and with a thunderous boom that sent shocks through the air, the can which he was still holding in his hands, exploded. Ishmael was immediately engulfed in flames, and before he could extinguish the fire about him, most of his clothing was burned clear off his body.

He finally, after struggling for what felt like minutes, put the fire completely out, but not before he was burned on the torso, arms, and a good portion of his face. He was in extreme pain, screaming at the top of his lungs for help of any kind, not knowing what would bring him immediate relief.

When a neighbor heard the wicked cries through the window to the rear of the home, he quickly ran from his house, and over to where he could hear a man sobbing in apparent pain. He followed the noise to the kitchen, and not knowing what else to do, kicked the door open to find Ish lying on the floor, arms spread out wide, looking helplessly up to the ceiling. It was as if he was crying to God wondering why him.

The man quickly told Ishmael to hold on, and he hastily summoned a local doctor who thankfully was able to bring some relief to Ish. They then called on a doctor familiar with burns, a Doctor Miller of Radnor, which was actually close to the town Ish was raised in.

That doctor and the neighbor looked around to see what had caused such terrible burns to this poor unfortunate fella, and quickly saw that an oil can had been completely flattened as if it were a simple sheet of paper. This, they discovered, was the cause of the tremendous boom.

The Doctor, who dressed Heald's wounds to protect the burns, was baffled that this man could survive such an incident and that the home was somehow not set ablaze and engulfed entirely.

It just seemed to add to the mystique of Big Ish, who no matter what happened to him or around him, could not be counted out, ever. It would take weeks for him to recover enough to go back home, and truthfully, after all the hard work he had done to secure some freedom, and after all the effort he had put into quitting alcohol and fighting, it seemed to matter none at all. He was ashamed of the incident and would decide he was better off amongst those he knew. For they, at least, were used to the strange things that seemed to always follow him.

Ish reached out to his former brother-in-law, Dennis Waters, and asked him if he had any room for an ageing, old steely, who just wanted to live the remainder of his days without causing a single issue further. As he told Dennis,

"I am spent of this life. I rather sit in peace from here on out, as long as the out may be."

Dennis did not hesitate, and insisted Ishmael get his things together, and head on over to his place. He would figure out a way to make his old friend comfortable, and Dennis' wife would be home to see to the bandages Ish would have for an extended time.

He was done with steel. There would be no way, with the damage the fire had done to his body, that he would be able to work with his hands in the manner needed. He was closing a chapter in his life without his say, and because of that, he felt a bit lost. He had known very little outside of steel work, and at least there he was well respected for his knowledge and strength, which men could only obtain through years of grinding and lifting.

As chance would have it, though, Dennis had heard of a job opening not far from where he lived. It was at the State

Hospital in the borough of Norristown, which housed the mentally ill from in and around the state. All he would need to do is see to it that the grounds were kept well, and if something decided to break, he would see to it that it was operational once again. He was still good with his hands, even if he did not have the strength to lift as he once had.

At first, Ish was unsure if this would be a good move for him, but ultimately, he figured it was a lot better than sitting around the house complaining about his ailments. Besides, it would allow him to stay busy, which was something he was accustomed to. In all his years, there was seldom a time when Big Ish was not working in one manner or another.

For the first few weeks, he got to know the other men working there, and learned his duties, as simple as they were. He enjoyed being outside in the fall air and working inside during the cold of the winter. This was a job he could do for the rest of his life, he thought to himself.

Perhaps life had finally thrown old Ish a bone and allowed him to carve out a peaceful spot on earth to call his, where he could enjoy things at last, without feeling as if he was always behind. Perhaps this was his time, after serving nearly fifty plus years of penance for a life he would do much differently if given a second chance.

Chapter 33

While staying at the home of Dennis Waters, Ish was able to reconnect with some old friends he had known through the years both in Conshohocken and Norristown, mostly through his work in the steel mills. These were men that had suspicious ways about them, but for a man like Ish, were understood more than most could ever understand.

Life wasn't easy growing up as these men had, and coming from fearful parts of town that forced you to be predator or prey brought a sort of comradery to men of the same nature. These were men that were certainly more of the predator nature in their heydays, but even for them, those same sands of the hourglass had to run down on their existence eventually. They were still tough as nails, as they say, having old man's strength, but they seldom went looking for a good scrap anymore when out and about. They much preferred the simpler life, knowing they need not throw hands if they decided not to.

These were men who had at times fought with Ish, and thankfully more often, alongside of him, earning them a respect so few men ever knew. They knew of the fight that Amos had with both Old Ish and Big Ish, and they knew of the concern Big Ish had over what had happened to his child out there on the streets of Philadelphia. They never believed for a second that his precious child, who was happier than most kids they knew, had harmed herself to the point of escaping this place. It just made no sense to them at all.

They had jokingly called themselves as the "Calvary of Suffering", referring to the difficulty each had in life. The men, although born from different parts of the area, and coming from Irish, English, and even one of Polish decent, were bound together by hard work and a harder way of living. They worked at mills throughout the area together, and drank from the same barrels during their down time. Alone, they had been formidable for sure. Together, they once were a danger to anyone who dared test them.

Ish had severed ties in some ways over the years, because he truly tried to lay low, but as the men aged, and as time was catching them all, he found himself looking for their friendship that went without question, and the loyalty that died only when each man breathed a final breath.

The common theme for them was that they could not stand the ways of men who rubbed them in the wrong manner due to their desire for selfish pleasures. Amos Alexander was one such man, and the Polish man, a man they nicknamed Pig Iron, had run-ins over the years with him on a few occasions. At times, Amos would get the better of the two, but there were times the stubborn Polish man would lay on a beating heavy enough against the formidable Amos, making for a sight to see and for respect to be gained.

Pig Iron had recently worked briefly in Reading where he saw Amos on a few occasions. They had no words, possibly because the men had grown to let old grudges die, or possibly because each had no more business to tend to with the other at this age.

But they knew just how Ish felt about the man he claimed knew more than he had mentioned when questioned back in 1899. They could tell that his fatherly instincts had smelled something awful in his story, a devilish line of lies that stretched for miles, and so they swore to Ish that if he ever wanted to see his end, they would happily oblige without question, and face the hell they had believed was an eventual state for each of them anyway.

But Ish knew, as loyal as the men were, things could point his way if they were ever caught. It could appear to be an accident for sure, but what if someone felt it was an act of revenge by a father who had somehow waited over a decade to gain it? Sure, there were plenty of men who despised Amos, but Big Ish wanted to keep the promise he made to those grandkids. He swore his days behind iron bars were in the past and that the only time he would ever leave them again would be in death. They would hopefully forget he ever had that stint as they grew older, and instead would remember a man who overcame such great odds, to straighten out a life most would see as a waste of time.

Besides, the State Hospital job was working out well, and he had more downtime than he had when working in the mills. Those long twelve-to-fifteen hour days were now a thing of the past, and he could enjoy the daylight left to visit with his son and the kids, while still feeling awake enough to enjoy it.

The pay was not what it had been while out west, but it did not matter. He was living a simple life, no longer caring about living a life filled with the comfort of being alone, and with his drinking days behind him, he just did not care for much of anything. He paid a small share of his earnings to Dennis and his wife, but aside from that, there was little to worry about. He had even given up his favorite flask, one he had a friend make for him years before, giving it to that Polish friend of his.

William and Annie seemed to be on a break from having children, but as Annie said once before,

"I am not finished bringing beautiful babies into this world. Not by a mile," smiling as she said this.

William was fine with whatever she wanted. He was loyal, and cared only for what she wanted in life. Ish truly admired his son for the ability to love as a man should, but rarely could. He was living the life he had wanted but could never afford, for his actions caused him to lose more than they allowed him to gain. Yet, still, he smiled through his pain as he realized a pattern of sorts had been halted from a line of life that was handed down with intention.

Ishmael was also lucky enough to be able to use some time off from his new job, and as luck would have it, two weeks were granted to the big man. He had no idea what he should do with those days free, but he did not care much about that. What was important was that he would have time to heal his body some, especially the burns he suffered most recently.

Dennis told him he should take a few days and visit friends out in the Harrisburg area, but Ish wasn't so sure. He wasn't feeling himself entirely, so he felt staying a bit closer to home may be the best way to spend that time off. Besides, it was hard for him to be down for so long. He had rarely had time off like this in his life, so he did not want to feel the pressure of boredom, which had led to so many drunken fights over his lifetime.

But one afternoon while walking to meet up with his son, Ish felt a terrible pain that buckled the giant of a man hard to the ground below. He grabbed at his stomach, clutching it tightly with both arms. At first, he thought maybe it would go away, and he would simply finish his walk to his son's and worry about it at another, more convenient time.

Only the pain did not subside, but instead intensified tremendously. He was alone but did not for a second think to get help from anyone he knew. He was not one to burden people if he could help it, and besides, he could just walk on over to Charity Hospital and have it checked out quickly.

By the time he arrived at the front doors, he was nearly

passed out from the searing pain, screaming in an agony he had never known. This tough, stubborn, old mass of a man was brought down to his knees by a pain he could not explain. He was suffering at this point so terribly that when the doctors asked him to explain what he was feeling, he could not other than to say it was bad for sure.

He was admitted and became seriously ill in a short amount of time. Upon further investigation, it was determined that he was suffering from internal hemorrhages. The doctor began to ask Ish what type of injury he may have had, as it seemed to be the only logical reasoning for his condition. But by this time, he was simply too sick and in too much pain to be able to speak, and so he did not.

Word got out to his brother William, who immediately told Ish's son and his wife what was going on. Both his brother William and his son, William, headed out to visit with him, and to see what they may be able to do to help him out.

In true Ish fashion, he tried to make it out to be nothing more than a bruise inside that somehow had refused to heal properly, but he knew it was much more. His brother had spent much of the day talking with doctors and ensuring that when his nephew William had to go, that he could get word to him if anything changed.

During the stay, there were a few times when Ish was able to mutter a few words, but for the most part, he lay silent, trying to control the agonizing pain that was within his old body.

At one point, he turned to see his police officer brother

sitting there in uniform, almost as if he were watching guard over him. Ish took that moment to ask his brother a question.

"William, do you suppose that when we die and meet our maker, that there were times He was busy doing other things and didn't notice when we were doing those things we ought not to have been doing?"

Wiliam knew his brother was scared, unsure of what lay ahead when his day would come. He understood that any man who had done wrong in his life would have that same fear, but for a man that had troubled others as much as Ish had, he truly did not know the answer.

"I am unsure of what to expect, brother, but I know this. Not everyone that does wrong, intended to do wrong. Sometimes, when I talk with a criminal, I understand that it wasn't an intent to do evil, but more of a necessity in their minds. So, what you have done in life, was it a necessity or was it meant to harm?" William asked.

Ish turned away for a moment, wondering for the first time, had he lived his life the way he had on purpose, or because it was just the way it had gone? He was unsure, but he knew what William meant. The good news, though, was that he had time to change. If he could adjust a few more things, perhaps God would have mercy on him, and know he really wanted to spend eternity in His house.

Then two days later, on Wednesday, a man, who some would swear was a myth had they not set eyes upon him, witnessed his commanding presence, or heard his powerful voice, finally passed on from this earth. A man who had seen and done things that would surely kill most other mortal men, and had lived a life full of pain, died a painful death. But now, as his family prayed for his soul, he would spend eternity with having to deal with no more pain. He was, after all, a man who had made mistakes for certain, but one who had done right by others as well when he could.

His official cause of death was noted as esophageal cancer and hemorrhaging. Of all the things that should have killed this man, it was not what could be seen, but what was unseen that finished him off.

He had every right, young William felt, to see his Mary Agnes again, and to maybe even see Grace to let her know how sorry he was that he could not be a better husband to her when she needed it most. If she forgave him, perhaps they could spend some time together, doing the things they had always wanted to.

But no one knew for certain if Ish would make it through those gates or find himself somewhere very different.

Wherever he was, they knew he could no longer feel the pains he had suffered here for fifty plus years of life. He was free of that, at the very least.

Life would need to go on as it had when Grace passed on, with or without anyone's permission. But a man that had secured a particular place in time, even though he never knew it, was going to be mourned as he should.

Chapter 34

* * *

There are days we live wondering just how and when our time will come, when it will run short. Is it better to see it coming so that we can say our proper goodbyes, and perhaps finish up those things we need to tie up so they were completed? Would we grant some needed forgiveness whether asked for it or not, knowing that as we leave this world for another, it would be surely better to not carry that weight with us any longer?

For Ish, he may have known that when he entered that hospital, it would be the final time he would see the sunshine on his feet, or feel the rain falling peacefully onto his head, as he looked up and thanked the clouds for sending him water to clear his face of the dirt and grime from a long day's work. He probably figured he would never taste another drop of alcohol, but who knows? Maybe he was glad he had conquered that feeling, even if only for a short time in his life.

His brother had lost so many people over the last decade

and a half, but losing his brother and wife so close together made him struggle for a time. He never wanted Ish to feel as if he was disappointed in him for the life he chose or perhaps the one that chose him. Even for a man as straight as an arrow as William, he knew not everyone could be gifted the same sight in life. Ishmael could have felt that in his heart of hearts, he was doing the very best he could possibly do for himself.

His son had lost both of his parents and seen a family he was raised in wiped out just as if it never existed. But he was proud of the man his father was, if only for the fact that he never stopped trying to be better, do better, and love better. The grandkids would lose a man that others feared, but that they never did. He was both the hardest and most gentle man, depending on who you were.

His funeral was not heavily attended, but those that were there, were there for the right reasons. People he had loved as best he could, and those he had been there for in time of need, stopped by to say a final farewell. It was interesting to see a mountain of a man looking so peaceful and calm as he lay there for one last look.

Ish was buried next to his father, in an unmarked grave as he requested. His father had asked for the same sixteen years prior. The reason those closest to him felt, was that he wanted to leave this world behind for good. Having a place where those who loved him and those who hated him could visit him whenever they wished, didn't make a lot of sense to him.

So he was granted that final wish. A place to rest, undisturbed, for the rest of eternity. A selfish way to be alone, perhaps, but an unselfish way to tell others he did not feel as if he was anyone to cry over.

After a few months of getting back to the grind of life, his brother was seated in the same chair he sat in each morning and each night, the same one he talked to his loving wife Mary in, and the same one he spent hours trying to convince his stubborn brother of a better life to come if he would just make some adjustments.

A headline a few pages deep into the newspaper caught his attention as if it were calling his name in bright letters. His eyes were fixated, reading the words that some reporter had come up with to describe something of great interest.

The headline began,

"Suspect Foul Play".

For a police officer, he knew all too well that this meant someone had died, and usually by the hands of someone who had it out for them. He would read on, just to see if perhaps it was someone he knew, or at the very least, something interesting to a law enforcement officer.

As he read, his eyes grew as wide as saucers, as he knew exactly the man being referenced. William could not believe what he was reading.

It read,

"July 31: Foul play is suspected in the death of Amos Alexander, fifty years old, who came here several years ago from Norristown, PA. and whose body was found early today lying along the railroad track at Wernersville, above Reading."

The article went on to explain that it was first thought Amos was hit by a passing train as this often happened when someone was drunk and not paying attention, but that the peculiar position in which he was found in, made authorities think a different tale.

The nature of the wounds also suggested that he may have been killed in some other manner, as the injuries were not consistent with that of a train accident.

It was determined by those same authorities that Amos was known to have had enemies in the area recently, who were growing jealous of his attention to a woman who lived not far away.

William knew that it would be near impossible to find the man or men responsible for such a death if there were no witnesses, and no one would talk about it. People tended to mind their business in situations like this, especially for a man who had few friends and more enemies.

The death of such a bad man did not totally surprise William, but the timing was interesting. He had only buried his brother a few months prior, and as luck would have it, Amos joined him shortly after.

William knew that the men Ish had been friends with for so long had gone back and forth to the Reading area for work, but he knew if they had anything to do with the crime, no one would ever know. Loyalty ran deep with certain folks, and if they had a hand in this, it was strictly because they felt the need to give one back for Ish's sake.

But it would turn out that the investigation would be short, as it was when Mary Agnes had passed. The police report would state that the coroner suspected no foul play after all, despite the mysterious wounds to his body. They wrote that he had most likely slipped while trying to steal a ride back home, and that was his demise.

The rumors, they concluded, had all been run down to find no factual evidence of a jealous group of men who had hatred for Amos over a woman. They believed that rumors had been started to make it seem more dramatic, or perhaps to throw the authorities off another trail, but this came after only one day of investigating.

William knew it was hard to prove much, and the departments wanted to close cases as quickly as they had opened them. Leaving too much unfinished created a backlog that no department wanted to deal with.

Amos's body was returned home to the Norristown area, and he was soon buried in the same cemetery as both Ishs were. It was an interesting place to bury a man who had such enemies in life. They could now be enemies in death if they so chose.

So much suspicion had surrounded both Amos and Ish, as both men had been tied to each other without wanting to for decades. They had occasionally fought one another, as one interrupted a family in ways no man should ever do. They came from the same line of hard work and long days, and even longer nights when they drank. This played a factor in their lives outcome.

But by the end of the month, in the year 1916, it was over. No one would ever know what had really happened to Mary Agnes, nor would anyone know what had truly happened to Amos Alexander on those cold tracks. Both were deemed horrible accidents, but truthfully both had so much surrounding their deaths, that few would agree with what the authorities had surmised.

Even William, who spent years in law enforcement and had seen his share of questionable deaths followed by quick investigations and even quicker drawn reports, questioned both deaths. He knew that there was more to both stories, but there was nothing he could do to prove his theories.

Ultimately, one had to wonder if Big Ish had in fact gotten his final revenge. Much like the way he lost the leg from the knee down, Amos had lost, too, only much more. It was less than three months after Ish's death and the circumstances surrounding the men Ish had reunited with recently, the manner in which Amos fell to his death, and the timing, all caused pause.

Perhaps revenge was received, or it was truly a coincidence. Either way, Amos was no longer able to hurt another as he had so many times over the course of his life. Perhaps he, too, battled the demons that Ish did for many years. It could simply be that he was a selfish, simple person who did not care for life the way others did.

But it was over, and life continues on, as it must, with a few less characters to watch as it did.

The End

As stated at the start of this story, Ishmael Heald Junior was very much a real man who lived a life that most of us would probably not have been able to survive and continue on as he did.

He was troubled for certain, and had made many bad decisions over his time here on earth, but I believe he had suffered from a life that demanded too much from him at times, and turned him into something he did not necessarily wish to be.

Had he been the size of most typical men, he may have rode under the cover of normalcy and not stood out like a sore thumb. He could have found that a plain, simple life was better suited to enjoying the fruits of his labor, but that was not the case for him.

He found alcohol to be an escape from both pain and reality, and while it probably allowed him some peace while he was enjoying a few drinks, it haunted him when he got to the point of no return.

We judge others so often for the way they live their life, but seldom do we get to understand the miles they had to walk through over rough terrains that we did not. The stumbles along the way are typical for us all, but for some, those stumbles come with speed that tears away the path we were intended to follow and we never find our way back.

I knew very little of Ish before I started my research, and what I found amazed me for sure. He had made the papers so often over a hundred years ago, but rarely for good reasons. I was told stories as a child of my great-great grandfather who somehow lost a leg at some point when he was young, and for some reason tried to drown a man in a horse trough during a fight.

I knew his last name to be different than mine is today, but with heavy research, and a vague memory of my father mentioning the different last name when I was a child, I found it. His obituary states that Ishmael Heald, father of William Hill, passed away suddenly. It was the missing piece I needed to prove he was one and the same.

That led me on a chase to find more of this man they called, "Big Ish."

I cannot for certain say he meant well, but I can say for certain that he gave this life hell. Even if he had made many mistakes throughout his travels, he also worked harder than I will ever need to, and he overcame greater odds than I could dream of. He was a legend to me in my younger years, but as he came alive again during the time I wrote this story, I could even see him almost as if he were sitting there next to me, watching as I wrote his story as best I could.

If I had to guess, he figured that when he died, no one beyond a generation would ever remember him. His grandchildren were young when he passed, and not all of them had been born yet. His only remaining relatives outside of them were his brother, William, and his son, young William.

One man and one woman produced two children, of which only one had children of their own. Otherwise, a line would be gone and I would not be here to tell his tale.

My own grandfather, James J Hill SR., was not born

until 1919, three years after Ishmael had died. He may have heard stories told by his father, William, of how he battled men and always seemed to come out on top. Maybe there was the tale of how he lost his leg in that gruesome train accident, and how instead of screaming and begging for help, he told those around him to let him be, for he was alright and just a bit saucy.

My father, James Junior, has a memory unlike most people I know. Without him remembering the stories told by his father and uncles, I would not have had any desire to know this man more. It was the incredible tales that caught my attention, and made the truly larger than life man entirely real and someone I wish I had had a chance to meet.

William and Annie had a total of nine children, including my grandfather.

Marion, who was the first born, died in 1946 at the age of 41. She had brain hemorrhaging and as the story goes, was beaten by her husband many times, and at some point, forced to live under her front porch. She had a tough life unfortunately and died a terrible death.

Carroll was a well-known singer in the Norristown area and made records during his time. He had a tremendous voice, but just like Ish, he fell in love with the devil's drink. One night while coming home from a night of heavy drinking, he fell down a flight of stairs and broke his neck. He lived with the broken neck until his death in 1958 at the age of 50.

Elizabeth married and lived a long life, dying at the

age of 79. Lawrence lived until 1987, and followed in the footsteps of his uncle William, working as a prison guard for much of his life.

Then there was William, Frederick, and Joseph, as well as James Sr., who were all born after the death of Ish.

Frederick stood at six feet, six inches tall, and started his career off as a motorcycle cop in the same town Ish spent many years living and fighting in Norristown, PA. He eventually ran for Sheriff of Montgomery County and won.

As for Ish's brother, William, he was elected to the position of Chief of Police of Conshohocken, and worked until almost the hour he died. He had gone to work, not feeling himself, and eventually was talked into going home to rest. He died that evening, in the year 1928. He is buried in New Saint Matthew's Cemetery, with just the simple words, "W Heald," on his stone.

His line stayed Heald, but with none of the boys producing any children. So the name died there.

Ishmael had twenty-six great grandchildren, and over fifty great-great grandchildren.

His line has produced successful people in a Doctor, a Singer, a Sonographer, many that own their own businesses, and veterans of WWII, Korea, and Vietnam. It produced hard-working men and women who raised families of their own. It even produced an author, who was completely humbled by retelling his story.

His memory will live on because he was important enough to find again, and the lessons he taught without meaning to, are invaluable. They show what a person can overcome, but also what a person needs to watch out for. Life is meant to be lived to the fullest, but with balance. If we learn a lesson from him, it would be to live with a healthy balance, and not with an unhealthy, reckless disregard for what comes from our actions.

It's been over a hundred years since he walked the same dirt we walk in our lives and through the same neighborhoods with many of the same houses still standing, and who knows? Someone just might find our simple existence to be anything but simple a hundred years from now, and our story could be told, keeping us very much alive, longer than we ever imagined we would be remembered.

Pictured seated is Ishmael Heald Jr., otherwise known as "Big Ish", on the right standing tall, Marion Hill, in front of her, Carroll F Hill, and seated on his lap, Elizabeth Hill. Circa 1912

Leg Crushed under a Car.

The Lancaster *Intelligencer* of Tuesday says that a man who gave his name as Ishmael Heald and says his home is in Conshohocken, Montgomery county, was brought to this city late last night minus a great part of one leg, which he lost in a railroad accident. About 8 o'clock last evening Christian Snyder. of Columbia, a track walker in the employ of the Pennsylvania railroad, was walking along just east of St. Charles furnace, which is west of Columbia, when he discovered a man lying along the south track of the railroad. He examined him and found that he had been badly injured, one leg having been crushed. The man was taken to Columbia, where the limb was amputated just below the knee, by Dr. Craig. Afterwards the man was brought to Lancaster on a freight train, which arrived here at exactly 12 o'clock, and he was taken to the county hospital, where he is doing very well to-day.

The accident happened when the man was trying to board a freight train for the purpose of stealing a ride, and it was largely owing to the fact that he was intoxicated. He was very drunk when found by Snyder, and remained in that condition for a long time afterwards, although he was pretty well sobered up by the time he reached Lancaster. When questioned by the persons having him in charge after the accident he was very saucy and not only refused to tell what his name was or where he hailed from but cursed everybody about him. To-day he has much more sense, as he realizes how badly he is hurt and what a narrow escape from death he had. He is about 26 years of age.

The injured man was brought to this city in the caboosse of a freight train, and it was with the greatest difficulty that he was taken out and placed on the old stretcher that has been in use at the station for many years. He was finally put into the wagon which is used for carrying the mails from the station to the postoffice, which rattled off over the rough streets to the hospital.

Carroll F Hill during his tour
in World War II.

Dennis Waters, the large
trackwalker, and Ish's brother-in-law.

Catherine Curran Waters, Dennis'
wife, who took Ish in before he died.

Lawrence Kelley, Annie Kelley Hill's
father, who died in 1899
from consumption.

In the middle, Marion Hill Troilo, right before she died. Annie is to her left with the printed dress.

Grace Waters Hill when she was a child.

Marion Hill Troilo before she was sick.

From left to right, Joseph Hill, Annie Kelley Hill, James J Hill Sr., and William Hill, Ishmael's son. Unknown standing in the rear.

The Philadelphia paper posted this only known photo of Mary Agnes Hill, Big Ish and Grace's daughter, right after her death in 1899.

A photo of the Conshohocken police force. In the back row, to the right with the thick mustache and glasses, is William Heald, Ishmeal's brother, who became the towns Chief of Police.

Pictured standing in the rear is William Hill, and from
left to right:

Annie Kelley Hill holding Lawrence, Ishmael holding
Carroll and Elizabeth, and Marion standing. Circa 1914

If you enjoyed this story, be sure to check out the Authors other novels, available on eBook, paperback, and hardback.

When the Dandelions Sing

"When The Dandelions Sing," is a warm, heartfelt story about a young boy named Ronnie Jefferson McFarland Jr., who is trying to understand the meaning of the word "purpose", and what his purpose is in life.

His grammy, who nicknames him Jasper for some reason known only to her, and his grandad, give him valuable lessons through their own eyes, and a window to the past that sometimes gets overshadowed by bigger things in life, but never truly forgotten.

While Ronnie's momma struggles with her life, he leans on others around him to gain perspective and a sense of understanding. He learns that even after people leave his world, their impact remains, and he never stops learning from them. As it turns out, some of the best lessons in life come from those who seemingly have nothing left to give.

Ronnie learns that a family is not always conventional, but oftentimes made up of the people you choose for yourself, and who choose you in return. He discovers that joy can be found in the smallest of things and the simplest of moments…for even among a field of perfect flowers, the simple dandelion can sing.

"Everything has purpose, and everything, a meaning beyond what we are even meant to understand. That's just the way it is. Purpose is not what we want it to be. It's simply what is meant to be."

Phoebe's Heart of Stone

In 1919, an unthinkable tragedy struck the blue-collar town of Alliance Ohio, and one particular family, the Bradway family, found themselves at the center of its terrible wrath. In the wake of disaster, Carl, a father of six, was forced to make a decision that would affect both himself and those he loved for the rest of their lives.

Carl and his beloved wife, Phoebe, had worked tirelessly to build a life of love and contentment for themselves and their six young children. Though determined and deeply in love, the young family could not escape the horrible black cloud that haunted their family, seemingly hell-bent on taking all they had built together.

This story follows the shocking true-life events of a family who wished for the simple things in life, but instead faced a path riddled with misfortune that altered the course of each of their lives forever.

The Gift of Life, Plus One

Agnes is a young, unconventional little girl, who wants to be exactly who she is. Her father, Jon, struggles with the balance of raising his children the way he sees fit, while still allowing them to grow into the people they are destined to become.

When Agnes suddenly falls ill, her life and the lives of those around her are altered forever, in ways they never imagined. Both her father and mother, Amanda, are faced with challenges that will either break them, or save them.

Jon finds that when he drifts off to sleep, his mind often travels to a unique place where he is mostly alone with his thoughts, while discovering that accepting life is not always easy, but important to moving on to the next season of life.

"The Gift of Life, Plus One," provides the perspective that just because life doesn't necessarily go as we planned, it's exactly the way it was intended to go.

The Forgiving Path to the City of Springs

A young, often brash Michael Kelley is a tough, South Philly man with a dislike for anyone who cannot push through the struggles life throws your way. His past was riddled by tragedy and a poor upbringing, which he has allowed to shape him, for good or for bad.

He finds himself in front of a judge who offers him two options. Go to jail to serve his sentence, or agree to do community service within the city limits. He agrees to the community service, but has no idea of what is in store for him.

When Michael finds himself in the Mudflaps Tent Community for the Homeless along the Schuylkill River, in the very city he was raised in, he quickly wonders if he chose wisely. He loathes the homeless with a bitter rage for all they represent in his mind, and now must help those same lost souls.

But meeting two men, Von, who resides within the community but doesn't seem to fit in, and Marcus, who works for a nonprofit that helps the homeless and seems better suited to live there than Von, Michael quickly realizes he may have misjudged. Now he must decide if he can forgive others in his life, or if it's perchance him he needs to forgive.

The Forgiving Path to the City of Springs (98,700 words) is a novel told from the perspective of one Michael Kelley, and at times reflects on a horrible past he would rather forget, but cannot, or perhaps should not. This book gives a unique perspective on finding hope, learning to see deeper and clearer than your eyes allow, and ultimately, granting forgiveness.